j
c.1

    Krensky, Stephen.
      The witching hour. Illus. by A.
    Delaney.   Atheneum, c1981.
     155 p. illus.

     Sequel to: The dragon circle.

   I. Title

50048994
  9.95   81-001398/AC

The
Witching
Hour

The Witching Hour

by *Stephen Krensky*

ILLUSTRATED BY A. DELANEY

J

C.1

Atheneum *1981* *New York*

For Frederick Wagner

LIBRARY OF CONGRESS CATALOGING IN PUBLICATION DATA

Krensky, Stephen.
The witching hour.

Sequel to: The dragon circle.
SUMMARY: The Wynd family pit their forces against
a group of witches with a ghastly plan to turn
the town's children into monsters.
[1. Witches–Fiction]   I. Delaney, A.   II. Title.
PZ7.K883Wi   [Fic]   81-1398
ISBN 0-689-30848-5   AACR2

The
Witching
Hour

ONE

JAMIE WYND stood in the middle of the living room, surveying the broom and dustpan at his feet. A determined look settled on his round face. "It should work this time," he muttered.

Frowning in concentration, Jamie began to move his hands over the broom. The straw twitched reluctantly. The handle shuddered. Then, like some fallen marionette about to perform, the broom rose up on end.

Jamie brushed back a curl from his forehead. "So far, so good," he said. He knew, however, that this bit of magic was nothing special. Oh, it might surprise some people, but his brothers and sisters could all do the same. Magic was more than a hobby with the Wynd family; they had practiced it for centuries.

It was a tradition Jamie was trying to enlarge

upon. He made a wide sweep with his arm, beckoning the broom across the floor. The broom responded, whisking once over the rug. "Gently, gently," Jamie murmured, his hands mimicking an orchestra conductor's.

The broom, though, was no longer paying attention. It spun around the room with alarming speed, raising dust with great efficiency.

From the top of the second floor landing, Jennifer and Perry Wynd watched the display through the banisters.

"I thought he'd get it right this time," whispered Perry.

"He should," giggled Jennifer, twirling a strand of her blond hair. "When I'm fourteen, I'll be able to manage it. I've got two years left to practice." She shook her head. "What a mess he's making."

"Should we go down?"

"Not yet, dummy. This could get better."

Jamie was quickly losing patience with the wayward broom. It may have been enjoying itself; he was not. Dust blew in his face. Coughing twice, he broke the spell.

The broom dropped like a felled tree.

Jamie debated his next move as the dust settled. If he gave up now, he would have to clean the living room himself. There was little chal-

lenge and no fun in that. But he would have to make some adjustments. Perhaps the dustpan would be more cooperative.

He motioned to it. The dustpan waited at his side while he swept under the coffee table. When he stopped, it gathered up the pile of dust and emptied it into the wastebasket. Jamie looked pleased. He moved on to sweep under a chair. The dustpan started to follow, but a milk-weed floated by and distracted it. Forgetting all else, the dustpan took off in pursuit.

Jamie was soon aware of the change. The dustpan was darting from room to room, career-ing around obstacles like a stock car in a road rally.

Jennifer nudged Perry. "You see," she hissed. "I told you it would get better."

Jamie was also delighted. The dustpan nego-tiated hairpin turns with great skill. He was busy applauding when the dustpan nicked the wall. Momentarily off balance, it wobbled back-ward, knocking over a small table that sup-ported a porcelain vase.

"That's Mother's favorite!" Perry gasped.

Both he and Jennifer gestured instinctively. The air filled with soft objects pulled from every corner of the house. The vase landed safely on a jumbled collection of sofa cushions, pillows, and a stray life preserver.

The dumbfounded Jamie regained his composure enough to stamp on the rug.

The dustpan settled to the floor like a dazed butterfly.

Jamie wagged a finger toward the stairs. "You two were spying on me," he said accusingly.

"And you're lucky we were," huffed Jennifer. "You're lucky we were." She and Perry slid down the banister. "If that vase had broken, Mother would have skinned you alive."

Perry frowned. "Mother wouldn't do that, Jen. She'd be mad, but not —"

"Quiet, you dolt." Jennifer clenched her fists. "I was using a figure of speech. Have you no imagination? Your brain is no bigger than a dinosaur's. It's a wonder you're not extinct." She paused. "What's that funny smell?"

Jamie laughed. "There's smoke coming out of your ears."

"What?"

Perry beamed at her. "It suits you," he said. "You were angry, so. . . ."

"Why, you little—"

"Before you two get started," said Jamie, "tell me why you interfered with my experiment."

Jennifer waved away the remaining wisps of smoke. "I told you already," she said. "Because the vase would have broken."

"I could have fixed it with magic."

Perry shook his head. "Not for long. It's Mother's favorite. You know she likes to look at it closely. The vase would fall apart whenever she touched it."

Jamie had forgotten that. Their mother, Elizabeth, had the unique gift of being immune to magic in any form. She could do none herself, nor could any spell affect her. Her children would not have wished that gift on themselves. Fortunately, they had inherited their father's skills. Alexander Wynd's family had magic in its blood.

"I suppose you're right," Jamie conceded. "But now the place looks more like a sultan's palace than a country house."

"It's better this way," Perry remarked. "A sultan's palace is more suitable for a pirate."

Jennifer groaned. "Don't even mention that word. I can't believe you're going to be a pirate again on Halloween. This is the seventh year in a row. It's embarrassing. Ever since you were three, you've been the terror of the seven seas. What kind of disguise do you think it makes? The whole town of Westbridge must know your 'Yo, ho, ho!' by now."

"I hope the whole state of Massachusetts

knows," Perry replied. "I like being a pirate. Besides, I make changes in my costume."

Jamie put the vase back on the righted table. "I doubt," he said, "that switching the patch from eye to eye counts as a change."

"It should."

Jennifer looked up in despair. "Why do I bother trying? You're being a dope, Perry. I'll bet Mother would—"

"I'd rather speak for myself," said Elizabeth Wynd, descending the stairs. Her eyebrows arched at the sight of the pillows. "I watched them fly by. Now I know where they went."

"Don't worry," Jamie said hastily, "we'll clean this up."

She smiled. "You certainly will. Now, Jennifer, what was it you'd bet I would say?"

"I was telling Perry that the purpose of Halloween is to disguise yourself. But he does all his trick-or-treating as a pirate. Everyone knows who he is."

Her mother's delicate features crinkled in thought. "I see," she said. "Everyone may not share your perspective, Jennifer. Perry do you agree with her about the purpose of Halloween?"

"Nope."

"Then what is it?" Jennifer demanded.

"To collect candy. Or cookies or brownies or even fruit."

"Oh, that," she sneered.

Mrs. Wynd tapped her nose. "As I recall, Jennifer, you never fail to compare your annual haul with Perry's."

"And she never wins, either," Jamie noted.

"That's because of her dumb costumes," Perry explained.

"Why, you little. . . ." A magic fireball flared up in Jennifer's hand.

Perry backed away.

Their mother stepped between them and put her hand over Jennifer's. "Let's calm down," she said. The fireball sputtered and went out. "I realize that few arguments in this house end pleasantly, but your father and I are tired of replacing Perry's charred sneakers. Show some patience, Jennifer. You can't get it from magic, but magic isn't always the answer. That goes for you, too, Perry."

"Edward's got patience," said Perry. "Maybe I could borrow his."

"Your big brother is not a bank," said Mrs. Wynd. "Where is he, anway?"

"Still at school," said Jamie. "Intramural soccer every Friday."

"That's right, I'd forgotten. And Alison?"

"She went into town after school," said Jennifer. "She wouldn't let me go with her. It's all very secretive. She's been like that a lot lately."

"It's a stage she's going through," Perry announced.

"And where did you hear about stages?" his mother asked.

"Well, last night on TV there was —"

Mrs. Wynd held up her hand. "You've answered my question. Try not to draw too many comparisons between TV and our lives."

"I'm glad I'm not going through a stage," said Jennifer. "It sure makes people grouchy."

"You're not?" said Perry. "Then what's your excuse?"

"Perry. . . ." Mrs. Wynd hustled him up the stairs. "Let's go work on your room. It's a disaster area."

"But I —"

"March. Jamie, you and Jennifer can put the pillows back."

She disappeared around the corner of the landing.

"Too bad," said Jamie. "You looked ready to clobber him."

"Oh, I will," replied Jennifer. "Time is on my side."

TWO

THE MAIN STREET of Westbridge, Massachusetts, was not bustling with people that Friday afternoon. Among those present, however, was Alison Wynd. She had on a tweed skirt and matching jacket, and her hair was pulled back into a bun. The tweed itched and the bun felt heavy, but Alison endured them both in the hope of looking older. Maturity, she thought, would help her get a suitable part-time job. And with a job would come money. Since school had begun, Alison had found her allowance sadly lacking. High school juniors somehow had a lot more expenses than sophomores. Her parents, though, had resisted giving her a raise. Faced with either spending less or working, Alison had chosen the latter.

But where to begin? The poster in the post office window heralded the arrival of Christmas stamps. Wasn't there a lot of mail at this time of year? An assistant or two might be needed. Squaring her shoulders, she opened the door and walked in.

"Good afternoon, Mr. MacArthur," she said.

A short, pudgy man with a genial air looked up from the counter. "Hello, Alison," he said. "How are you? You know, the Christmas stamps just arrived. You can have your pick."

"Thanks, Mr. MacArthur. Actually, I'm not here for stamps. I was thinking about Christmas, though."

"That's nice of you. My shirt size is sixteen-thirty-two. I like plaids."

Alison winced. This was not going the way she expected. "Um, I wasn't . . . that is . . . if I could begin—"

The postmaster laughed. "I was just teasing, Alison. What can I do for you?"

"Oh. I was wondering, with the Christmas rush and all, whether you might need an assistant."

Mr. MacArthur scratched his head. "Hard to say. Westbridge is no bustling metropolis, but I might."

"Really?" Alison was delighted.

"Of course, I'll have to find out who's available from the regional office in Springfield.

They keep the lists there of applicants who have taken the examination."

"Examination?"

He nodded. "Every prospective employee of the postal service has to take it."

"Can anyone take the exam?" Alison asked.

"Any high school graduate," Mr. MacArthur replied.

Alison sighed.

"Come back in a couple of years," Mr. MacArthur said encouragingly. "I'll still be here."

Alison could feel herself blushing. She said goodbye quickly and returned outside. She barely noticed the brisk wind blowing stray leaves over the sidewalk. "One down," she murmured, glancing around. Witherspoon's Hardware Store was across the street. "Who knows?" she said to herself. "It won't hurt to try."

A bell rang above her head as she entered. Mrs. Witherspoon greeted her at once.

" 'Afternoon, dear. How are you?"

"Fine."

"And your family? How are your parents getting on?"

"Well, thank you."

"Glad to hear it. So what brings you in, today?

It must be that old house of yours. Wouldn't live in one myself. You don't own them, they own you. But whatever the problem," she added, surveying her stock, "we've probably got the solution for it."

"Fortunately, Mrs. Witherspoon, the house is fine, too. I'm here for another reason."

"You're not selling raffle tickets, are you?"

"No, nothing like that."

Mrs. Witherspoon looked relieved.

"I'm looking for a part-time job."

Mrs. Witherspoon nodded. "It's good to see you showing some initiative. Too many young people have no thoughts of responsibility. How old are you now?"

"Sixteen."

"My, who would've believed it? I remember when your parents took you for strolls in a carriage. And now you're going to work. That's a big step. But it's never too early to learn what the world is all about. At your age, I'd already had three jobs. Looking at me now, I suppose, it's hard to imagine I was ever your age."

Alison's eyes passed quickly over Mrs. Witherspoon's plump figure and gray hair. "Not at all," she said politely. "I'm glad you know how I feel, though. By any chance is there a position open in the store?"

"Here?" Mrs. Witherspoon fidgeted with a box of screws. "It is true that Mr. Witherspoon isn't getting any younger. What kind of hardware experience do you have?"

Alison swallowed hard. "None, really. But I learn quickly."

Mrs. Witherspoon tapped her fingers together. "I'm afraid we could hardly make a place for a beginner. Mr. Witherspoon's nerves, not to mention my own, would not be up to it. I have the fondest regard for you and your family, but experience *is* experience."

"Oh," Alison said lamely. She wondered how people got their first jobs if they always lacked some previous experience. "I'd better keep looking, then. Goodbye, Mrs. Witherspoon. Thanks, anyway."

"Goodbye. And keep an eye on that house of yours. Something's bound to need fixing soon, mark my words."

Alison trudged out onto the sidewalk. Her afternoon was beginning to sour. Three stops later, she was very discouraged. Neither the grocery store nor the bookstore needed anyone at present, while at the clothing shop an opening had just been filled. Alison tried the library, too, but they had no funds to hire an intern.

As she walked back across the village green,

Alison glanced up at the fresh paint gleaming on the newly repaired church steeple. Almost everyone thought the steeple had been destroyed by lightning the previous spring. Only Alison and her family knew that a dragon had actually done the damage. A dragon that, along with four others, the Wynds had defeated.

Alison sighed. At the moment she would have preferred fighting dragons. At least then she could do something for herself. All she could do now was check the Westbridge Inn. She had avoided it so far, fearing that the only jobs there would be for chambermaids. Alison hated to make beds. Still, at this point she didn't have much choice.

"LET ME UNDERSTAND YOU, Miss Wynd," said the assistant manager, who doubled as a desk clerk. "You are sixteen years old. You have no hostelry experience. You have no driver's license, though you are studying to get a permit." He shook his head slightly. "You are, however, well-acquainted with Westbridge, having lived here all your life. I also gather that you dislike making beds."

Alison had not meant to be so transparent. "I'm willing to do whatever work is available," she insisted.

"*Willing?* What is *willing?* We at the West-bridge Inn have a long tradition of service to uphold." He touched both ends of his neatly trimmed moustache. "Do you think *willing* will keep your hospital corners sufficiently tight? Can *willing* put sparkle on a brass lamp or shine on a wood floor? I sincerely doubt it. The final decision should be the manager's, but he's out of town. Under the circumstances, I'm afraid. . . ."

"Excuse me," said a tall woman, standing by the window. She certainly looked businesslike, Alison thought. Her suit was impeccably tailored and her wavy hair fashionably cut.

"I'm sorry," said Alison. "I didn't mean to disturb—"

"Do I look disturbed?" the woman said calmly. "Let me introduce myself. I am Amelia Harding. My associates and I are holding a small conference here tomorrow, Sunday, and Monday." She glanced at the assistant manager. "But I am accustomed to establishments with far more staff than our present surroundings. You look like a capable girl. If you wish, I will hire you for the duration of the conference."

Alison barely managed to keep her mouth from falling open. "That's very kind of you, Miss Harding."

"Nonsense. I'm just being practical."

"Well, I appreciate the offer. I'd like to accept it, but Monday would be a problem. I know my parents won't let me skip school to work."

"How diligent of them," Miss Harding replied. "Actually, the conference activities will center around the evenings. If you can give up your weekend and arrive here directly after school on Monday, we'll manage nicely."

Alison smiled. "That'll be fine."

"Excellent. We have yet to discuss your salary, of course." She paused. The assistant manager was listening to every word. "Why don't you come to my room for a minute? We'll discuss it there. I see no reason for your earnings to be public knowledge."

Alison resisted the impulse to smile triumphantly and followed her new employer up the stairs.

THREE

LATE THAT SAME AFTERNOON, the subway exit near the Boston Public Garden disgorged an angular man with the spare look of a tree in winter. He turned sharply and strode toward the residential section of Back Bay. Despite the hint of Indian summer in the air, the man was hunched in a drab gray raincoat. He winced at the sound of passing laughter. Strangers were smiling at one another in the pleasant weather; his scowl remained frozen in place. Several dogs barked as he approached. The man subdued the temptation to kick them and walked on.

His destination was a tall, thin townhouse with shuttered windows and a mansard roof, distinguishable from its neighbors by the black paint covering its brick front. The man climbed the stone steps, entered an ornate anteroom, and pressed a key into the lock of the door. The key turned with a loud *click*. Shaking off all vestiges of the sunshine and high spirits outside, the man pushed open the heavy oak door.

"Who is it?" asked a high-pitched voice from the second floor.

"It is I, Madam. Nicholas Cudgel."

"Very well, Cudgel. I am in the library."

Cudgel breathed deeply of the musty air as he hung up his coat. He was careful to leave the dust on the hall table undisturbed. Both the air and the dust were the old lady's doing. It created an atmosphere, she said.

"Do not keep me waiting, Cudgel."

With an agility that belied his advancing years, Cudgel bounded up the stairs and entered the library.

"Good afternoon, Madam," he said respectfully.

The woman he addressed was sitting in a rocking chair by a marble mantle. Her face was lined like a furrowed field, framed by wavy white hair at its edges. A great white cat sat contentedly in her lap.

"October is warm this year," she observed, stirring the embers in the grate. The chair creaked under her weight.

"Indeed it is," Cudgel replied.

"Warm and inviting weather will serve our purpose well." She glanced up abruptly. "Confound you! Don't hover over me like that. I'm not some doddering old fool. Understand?"

"Perfectly, Mrs. Harding. I beg your pardon. I was only attempting to stoke the fire."

"Spineless, scheming. . . ." The cat moved restlessly. Mrs. Harding scratched it behind its ears. "There, there, Agatha. I did not mean for you to get upset."

Agatha hissed at Cudgel.

"Yes, yes, my pet. I'm sure that would prove interesting. But we need Cudgel. He's part of the plan. Aren't you, Cudgel?"

"I have tried my best," he said evenly, watching the cat with alarm.

"And he has worked hard on our behalf."

The cat's tail twitched once and then was still.

"But do not forget whose plan this is, Cudgel."

He bowed. "The plan is yours, Madam. And it is a brilliant one."

A crooked smile crept across Mrs. Harding's face. It was not a face that held smiles easily. "Quite right," she said. "You and Amelia are privileged to participate, as are the others. The secrets I have learned were recovered at great cost. I have sacrificed years of making mischief to delve into forgotten lore. Yet now I will be paid handsomely for my trouble. My name shall be remembered among the giants of our kind." She mumbled a word, and a fire blazed forth in the grate. "Tell me, what do you have to report?"

"Everything is proceeding smoothly. Miss Harding arrived in Westbridge this morning. The arrangements at the inn should be adequate."

"And the car?"

"It is being serviced. I will return for it tomorrow morning."

Mrs. Harding nodded. "A pity we must go to the bother. But arriving in the usual way might provoke untimely questions."

Cudgel hesitated.

"Is there something more?" she asked.

"Forgive me, Madam." He frowned slightly. "I have always admired your plan immensely, but one aspect of it has continued to puzzle me."

"You tread dangerously, Cudgel. Well, out with it!"

"I assure you, Madam, I mean no disrespect. I simply wish to learn from your wisdom. You see, I have wondered how you picked Westbridge for the, ah, experiment. It appears to be a rather insignificant hamlet."

Mrs. Harding pursed her lips. "Insignificant to the world, perhaps, but not to our purpose. Admittedly, it resembles dozens of other New England towns. Yet I have three reasons for choosing it. First, in such a remote place, we will find no interference. Second, a small community will be simpler for us to control once the plan has been realized. Third, and most important, last July, as I passed over the town while returning from a meeting in Albany, I felt the flow of Old Magic below. A great deal of energy must be expended for my plan to succeed. If we can tap the source of that magic, our task will be simpler."

Cudgel nodded, his curiosity at rest.

Mrs. Harding rose from her chair and hobbled to the window. Cars and people passed busily below. "Look at them," she sneered. "Bustling about over mortgages, new clothes, vacations, and birthday parties. The world has come to a sorry state. All my life I have lived with this frustration. But my moment, our moment, has arrived." She cackled hideously.

Cudgel smiled. Mrs. Harding's tone sent delicious prickles of anticipation tingling down his spine.

She continued to stare out the window. "The world has become almost foreign to our kind these last few centuries. Gone are the days when our advice was sought on every matter, days when we were feared and respected. Science has reared its grasping head since then, swallowing what it can comprehend and dismissing what it cannot."

"Current conditions are most unfortunate, Madam."

The cat jumped up to the window ledge, pressing its face against the glass and hissing at the crowds.

"We have been patient, Cudgel," said Mrs. Harding, stroking Agatha's head. "Perhaps too patient. Our forebearance is at an end. We will loose a plague among them, a plague that will return us to our former glory."

The grandfather clock downstairs struck four times.

Mrs. Harding turned from the window. "Come, Cudgel, it's getting late. And we still have the final preparations to make."

She walked slowly out of the library with Agatha at her side. Cudgel's face resumed his usual dour expression as he followed behind them.

FOUR

IT HAD TAKEN Perry most of the afternoon to find the dusty box he was now carrying into the living room. He placed it carefully on the floor and removed the top. The box was filled with wooden soldiers, each about six inches tall. Perry took out an infantryman and held it up to the light. The soldier was cunningly carved, its face firm and resolute, its uniform sleek and crisp. The paint, however, had worn away in several places; clearly the soldier had seen a lot of action. Perry put it down and removed another. This was a drummer, and unlike the infantryman it was unarmed. But the drum it carried was real.

Perry arranged the whole company in front of him and stepped back from their ranks. Now came the difficult part. These soldiers had been packed in the attic for years. He was not sure any magic would still rouse them. But he had hopes. . . .

The spell was a short one. As he finished it, Perry said, "I command you to walk."

The soldiers did not move.

Perry scratched his head. Was he doing it wrong or were the soldiers beyond waking? He went over the spell again. It had all been done properly. The soldiers should obey. He had given them an order. Or had he?

"Forward, march!" he shouted, with a military flourish.

The company responded at once. As the drummer set the beat, the soldiers crossed the rug, their arms and legs swinging in unison.

"Hooray!" cried Perry. His new position, though, allowed him little time to be pleased.

"Right face!"

The soldiers turned. They began a trek through the front hall in a box formation. Perry watched them parade back and forth, executing various drills under his direction.

Suddenly the front door banged open. The soldiers broke ranks, scurrying for cover under the radiator.

"Hi, Perry," Alison said cheerily.

"Look out!" he exclaimed, pulling her to the side. "You almost wiped out the troops."

Alison looked down. "Sorry," she said. "I wasn't expecting to find West Point in the front hall."

"Reassemble ranks," Perry called out.

The soldiers regrouped with hardly a glance at Alison. They were not afraid of her. Only the element of surprise had unsettled them.

"Drum roll," Perry ordered.

The drummer could muster nothing more than a slight tapping.

Perry knelt down for a closer look. "It sounded fine a minute ago. I wonder. . . . Oh, no! The drumhead's torn. It must have ripped in the confusion."

"Can you make a new one?" Alison asked.

"Not here," he said slowly. "But my art teacher might have the right stuff."

"Well, then, you can fix it at school on Monday."

"I guess."

"Good." Alison was not about to let Perry spoil her day.

Jamie poked his head around the corner. "Dinner in five minutes," he boomed solemnly, like Big Ben ringing in a new year.

Alison nodded. Feeling a little guilty about the drummer, she helped Perry put away the soldiers before she washed up.

THE DINING ROOM was a lively place during dinner. Dishes were passed around with alarming speed, voices rose and fell in no apparent pattern, and silverware clattered continuously. Elizabeth and Alexander Wynd refereed the occasion from either end of the table. For Alexander, a professor at nearby Berkshire College, the meal sounded much like the ones in the student dining halls.

"How was your game today?" he asked Edward, whose fork and knife were a blur of activity.

Edward swallowed. "Pretty good, Father," he said. "The other goalie played like a bag of doughnuts."

"Doughnuts?"

"Lots of holes," Jamie explained.

Edward nodded with his mouth full.

His father smiled. "Winning," he noted, "seems to improve your appetite."

Perry's appetite was not faring so well. He stared unhappily at the mountain of squash on his plate. Perry hated squash. Unfortunately, hating it did not help. The squash remained in plain view. Perry looked around warily. Nobody was watching him. He passed his hand over the squash and picked up his fork.

The motion distracted Jennifer. "Perry's at it again," she announced. "He's changed his squash into pudding."

Perry took a quick second bite. Before he could swallow it, the pudding turned back to squash in his mouth. He knew without looking that his father had done that.

Mrs. Wynd sighed. "Young man, I thought we settled this last time."

"Last time it was beets."

"You know what I mean."

Maybe he did and maybe he didn't. "I still don't see what harm the illusion does. I'm only fooling myself. The squash just looks and tastes like pudding; it hasn't really changed."

"Even so," his mother replied, "your magic should not be squandered on everything that doesn't suit your fancy. If you change whatever fails to please you at first, you will miss out on things you would have enjoyed in time. More importantly, it's the beginning of a dangerous habit. Someday, you might become unwilling to face any challenges at all. Do you understand that?"

"I suppose," he grumbled, wishing he didn't.

"You're such a baby," said Jennifer. "Squash is good. I love it."

Perry glared at her.

Jennifer smiled and stuck a large forkful in her mouth.

"Yuck!" she cried suddenly. "You may think you're being funny, Perry, but I don't enjoy having my squash taste like lima beans. I hate them, and you know it. But two can play at—"

"I think we've seen enough magic for one meal," Professor Wynd interjected. "And stop mumbling about revenge, Jennifer. You goaded him into it."

"But under the circumstances," Mrs. Wynd added, "I believe Perry deserves another helping of squash."

Perry's smirk vanished. Life was very unfair, he thought.

"If that's all settled," said Alison, "I have an announcement to make. I got a job at the inn today."

"Making beds?" asked Edward.

"Actually, I'm not working for the inn itself. I'm going to help out at a conference that runs through Monday."

"That sounds fine," said the Professor. "How big a conference will it be?"

"Thirteen people, Miss Harding said. She's the conference director."

"What will they be conferring about?" her mother asked.

Alison blushed. "I don't know. I was so pleased to get the job, I forgot to ask. Does that look bad? I'd hate to start off on the wrong foot."

"Don't worry," said Jamie. "By Monday you'll know more about it than you ever wanted to."

"Speaking of Monday," said Mrs. Wynd, "I trust you won't be missing any school."

"I thought of that, Mother. Miss Harding said she can manage without me until after school."

"Too bad," said Perry. "Missing school would have been the best part." He turned to his mother. "May I be excused?"

"Finish your squash, young man. Then we'll see."

A few minutes later, Alison and Jennifer helped clear away the dishes. Edward, Jamie, and Perry were already washing the silverware and glasses.

"Does this job mean you'll be busy Halloween night?" Jennifer asked.

"I'm not sure," said Alison. "It doesn't matter. I'm getting too old for Halloween."

"Not me. And this year I'm going to beat Perry for once. When can we work on my costume?"

Alison wrinkled her nose. "I did promise, didn't I?"

"Yes."

"Um, well, I won't be able to tonight. I've got to get ahead on my homework." She paused. "I probably won't have much time over the weekend, either."

"I see."

"Don't get huffy, Jen. I'm sorry. Besides, I'm sure you'll manage. And if you have any problems, you can ask—"

"Never mind," said Jennifer, heading for the stairs. "I don't need your advice. I'll do just fine on my own."

FIVE

THE NEXT MORNING was gray and cheerless. Outside the Westbridge Inn, Alison suppressed a yawn and shivered in her coat.

"Cold, Alison?" asked Miss Harding, who looked quite comfortable.

"Oh, no," said Alison, shifting her weight from one foot to the other.

Miss Harding nodded. "My mother will arrive soon. And she definitely likes to be met. Most of the other participants are already here."

"Is this a family gathering?"

"In a way. You might say that Mother is the keynote speaker." She smiled grimly. "I hope she approves of the arrangements. Mother is not easy to please."

Alison took a deep breath.

"Ah, here's someone now."

A taxi pulled into the drive. A tall woman

swathed in a long cape emerged from the back seat. Alison caught herself gaping. The woman's cape, hat, skirt, gloves, and boots were all black.

"Is she in mourning?" Alison whispered.

"Not at all," Miss Harding replied. "Jocelyn Grant is simply partial to black."

"She does look striking," Alison admitted.

Jocelyn Grant approached them at once, her heels clicking sharply on the flagstones.

"So glad you could come, Jocelyn," Miss Harding declared.

"Darling, I wouldn't have missed it. The invitation was just too intriguing." She turned her attention to Alison. "And who have we here?"

"This is Alison Wynd, a native of Westbridge. She's helping me during the conference."

"Indeed? Won't your mother be surprised, Amelia? Well, I'm sure you know your own business. How do you do, Alison?"

"Fine, thank you."

Jocelyn Grant looked around. "Where has Circe gone to? Circe! Circe! Come here for a moment."

A coal-black cat uncurled itself from the midst of Jocelyn Grant's luggage. Her fur was thick and shiny. Alison had never seen a cat with such big yellow eyes. Circe returned her stare without blinking.

"Ah, there you are. Circe was very pleased about this trip. She rarely gets to go hunting."

"Yes," said Amelia, "I can imagine her anticipation. Perhaps you'd like to go inside and freshen up. Lunch will be at noon in the Ethan Allen Room."

"The Ethan Allen Room?" Jocelyn laughed. "How quaint."

As Amelia Harding followed the porter and Jocelyn Grant inside, she passed the assistant manager coming the other way.

"Excuse me, Miss Harding," he said, "but I must speak to you."

"Yes?"

The assistant manager straightened his tie. "It's about the cats," he said.

"What about them?"

"Many of your conference members have brought them into the inn. This simply isn't done, Miss Harding. We've never had cats in the inn before."

"Then you're long overdue. Is that all? I'm extremely busy at present."

His jaw stiffened. "But this sort of problem cannot—"

"Problem?" The assistant manager now had her full attention. "Do I understand you correctly?" she demanded. "In what way are the

36

cats a *problem?*"

"You must know. . . ." He looked imploringly at Alison. "They're so cat-like."

Alison smothered a laugh.

"Perceptive of you," Miss Harding noted. "What do you propose doing about it?"

"The cats cannot stay in the rooms. They should sleep outside somewhere."

"Young man, must I remind you that I have a contract with the inn? We also paid for our rooms and meals in advance. And nowhere does it state that cats are forbidden on the premises. I made certain of that."

"Oh." The assistant manager fidgeted with a button. "Well, we assumed—"

"Incorrectly, it seems. I'm sure you wish to avoid any unpleasantness." She stared at him. "I believe the manager is returning later today. Perhaps I should bring up the matter with him."

"There's no need . . . I mean, that shouldn't be necessary."

Miss Harding smiled frostily. "Excellent. Then the matter is settled. We'll hear no more about the cats."

The assistant manager sighed. He felt a little dizzy. Citing some pressing business, he returned inside.

"One must be firm, Alison," Miss Harding

remarked. The sound of a car distracted her. "Ah, here's Mother."

Alison did not know what to expect from Mrs. Harding, but her car was certainly noteworthy. With its long hood, high fenders, and running boards, it looked like something from an old gangster movie.

The car stopped directly in front of them. Miss Harding walked forward to open the back door. "Hello, Mother," she said soberly. "How was your trip?"

"Uneventful," Madeleine Harding answered. She stepped out onto the flagstones and wrinkled her nose at the fresh air.

Her face made Alison think of prunes.

Meanwhile the driver got out as well. Alison thought of no fruits looking at him. His skin was stretched tight across his features, like the wings of a bat in flight. His eyes narrowed dangerously under Alison's glance. She turned abruptly back to the Hardings.

"Mother, I want you to meet Alison Wynd. She's a local girl I've hired to help with the preparations."

"Hello," said Alison.

Madeleine Harding looked her up and down with great deliberation. "How do you do?" she said finally.

Miss Harding motioned to the driver. "Cudgel, you must meet Alison, too. You'll probably be seeing a lot of each other."

"Pleased to meet you," said Alison.

Cudgel inclined his head slightly.

"But where is Agatha, Mother? Surely she came along."

"She was sleeping. Agatha hates to travel by car. She prefers to fly. Here she is now."

The largest white cat Alison had ever seen hopped out of the back seat. "What a beautiful cat," she said, bending over to pat it.

"Agatha doesn't take kindly to strangers," Miss Harding warned her.

Alison pulled back her hand.

Mrs. Harding looked a little disappointed. "Are we going to stand outside all day?" she asked.

"No, Mother, we'll be going in directly. Alison, I forgot to tell the other participants that lunch has been moved to the Ethan Allen Room. Could you see that they're told? I believe you'll find some of them in the sunroom."

Alison nodded. "I hope you enjoy your stay, Mrs. Harding. It was nice meeting you, Mr. Cudgel." She looked down. "And you, too, Agatha." She turned and went inside.

Madeleine Harding smoothed the wrinkles in

her gloves. "Is it wise," she said, "to have this girl assisting us?"

"The staff at the inn is less than ample. Besides, I had a delightful time making the clerk look foolish. And Alison is only a child. What could she possibly do even if she discovered something?"

Her mother grunted. "Well, I don't like her. She has two obvious faults—she seems happy and she's polite. I suppose she may be useful. But she is your responsibility." Madeleine took a deep breath. "I chose this place well. Can you feel the Old Magic? I sensed it most strongly as I stepped out of the car."

"We've been through this before, Mother. I don't have your sensitivity. Still, I'm glad you are so positive about it."

"Oh, yes, there's no question. A pity you didn't inherit that skill from me." She took another breath. "Now show me my room."

THE SUNROOM may have been aptly named, but on cloudy days it saw no more sun than anywhere else. Plants and wicker furniture covered the brick floor, the chairs arranged around glass-topped coffee tables. Near one such table two men and two women were seated. Both men looked to be in their sixties, though one was bald and bearded while the other had a mane of white hair and a walrus moustache. The women were clearly from different generations. One was young, with brown ringlets, deep dimples, and a pair of hoop earrings. The other had silvery hair, apple cheeks, and a pair of reading glasses perched on her nose. She seemed more intent on her knitting than on the conversation around her.

"The dryness of the straw is important," the bearded man remarked.

"And where it comes from," said the young woman, her finger tracing the edge of a dimple.

The second man nodded, though his hair stayed neatly in place. "Don't forget length," he noted. "In a strong wind, length makes all the difference."

"The handle is too often ignored," observed the older woman. Her needles clicked rapidly. "The variations in wood can be most significant."

It was the white-haired man who first noticed Alison standing by the door. "May we help you?" he asked.

"Excuse me," she said, "but are you here for the conference?"

They nodded.

"Miss Harding sent me to tell you that lunch

will be served in the Ethan Allen Room. It's a change in the schedule."

"Ah," the white-haired man continued, "you are working for Amelia. What's your name?"

"Alison Wynd."

"Well, let me introduce you to my colleagues. I am Nathaniel Mandrake. The dedicated knitter on my right is Sarah MacGregor. The bearded gentleman is Max Gunther, and sitting on his left is Phoebe Tokla."

Alison shyly exchanged greetings with them.

Phoebe giggled. "We were just discussing the makings of a good broom. Do you have an opinion on the subject?"

"Um, not really. I've mostly used vacuum cleaners."

Phoebe exploded in laughter. The others smiled.

Alison thought she must look like a ripe tomato. "I . . . I'm sorry to have interrupted," she said. "I'd better be getting on with my job."

She darted from the room.

"That was cruel, Phoebe," Max Gunther remarked.

"Yes," Phoebe said happily. "It was, wasn't it?"

"But hardly worth the bother," said Nathaniel. "Besides, we should be concentrating on the matter at hand. It appears none of us knows why we were called here."

"True," Max growled. "And I have urgent tasks awaiting me elsewhere."

Phoebe giggled again. "Don't we all," she noted.

"Come, come," said Sarah MacGregor, "we all know why we're here—because Madeleine Harding invited us. Which of you would dare refuse such an invitation? Everyone knows Madeleine's been working secretly on something for years. Perhaps she will now share her findings. Who knows? She may have other plans. We can be sure of one thing, though. If the Hardings are involved, whatever goes on is bound to be deliciously evil."

SIX

WHILE ALISON was busy at the inn that afternoon, Jamie and Jennifer were making their weekly trip to the Westbridge Public Library. The way through the woods was much shorter than the road, so naturally that's how they went. The rough path had its hardships, however.

"Hold on!" cried Jamie. He stopped to untie his sneaker. "I've got another pebble in my shoe. You'd think my feet were magnets or something, the way they attract them."

Jennifer shook her head. "It's your own fault. You drag your feet. I take light, feathery steps." She pranced about like a giddy ballerina, pirouetted sharply, and fell into a bush.

"I see," said Jamie, straightening up. "How nice of you to demonstrate."

"Hrrmph," was all Jennifer answered, pulling

the brambles from her sweater.

"That's easy for you to say. I'll bet—" He cocked an ear to one side. "Did you hear that?"

"Hear what?" she asked distractedly. For every bramble she removed, three barbs were left behind.

"That meowing. Listen! There it is again."

This time Jennifer heard it, too. "Cats," she said. After a moment, she added, "Unhappy cats."

Jamie frowned. "Do you think they're hurt?"

"Let's find out."

Tracing the shrill noise wasn't hard, even over the crunching of twigs and leaves at their feet. The two children quickly crossed a meadow and a small glen. Panting heavily, they came to the top of a ridge.

"Must . . . be . . . around . . . here . . . some-where," gasped Jamie.

"Down there," murmured Jennifer. She pointed to the gully below.

Five cats were gathered around a large milk can caught between two rocks. They were large cats, four of them black and one white. Their tails twitched repeatedly as first one and then another wailed loudly.

"You'd almost think they were talking to one another," said Jennifer.

"Look at those tracks," whispered Jamie. "Someone rolled that can the length of the gully." He shook his head. "Why would anyone do that?"

Jennifer shrugged. "Maybe it's a joke. Nobody would go to so much bother for a few gallons of milk."

"The cats might."

"Very funny. What do you really. . . ." Her mouth dropped open. "I don't believe it."

Three cats had begun pushing their heads against the top of the can. The other two cats were digging a hollow at the bottom. The can rocked forward and then fell back. Snarling, the two cats dug a little deeper. Then they tried again. One rock shifted a bit. The cats jumped back as the can tumbled loose and rolled a few feet.

"They're very well-trained," Jamie observed.

"I've never seen cats work together so carefully," said Jennifer. "It's like a circus act."

"They must really want the milk. Maybe they stole it."

"Don't be silly," scoffed his sister. "I've heard of cat burglars, but not burglar cats."

"The evidence speaks for itself."

Jennifer's protest sputtered out for lack of a better explanation. "However it happened," she said, "I suppose we should return the can to its owner."

"I guess so. I wonder whose it is."

"The owner's name is probably printed on the side. Come on, we may as well get this over with."

They slid down the wall of the ridge, scattering dirt and rocks ahead of them. The cats were not caught unawares. They sat between the can and the intruders. The white one hissed at Jamie.

"They're not glad to see us," he said. "And they sure look bigger from down here."

"*Fisher* is written on the can," said Jennifer. "Mr. Fisher's farm is just over the next hill. Sorry, kitties, but you'll have to step aside. It's nothing personal." She reached down toward the can.

The white cat swiped at her.

"Yeeooow!" she cried, jumping back in dismay. Two long red scratches lined her hand.

The other cats bared their teeth.

Jamie eyed them cautiously. "Are you all right, Jen?"

"I will be. Watch out for them, Jamie. They're mean."

"Shoo!" he shouted, waving his arms. "Go away! Scat!"

The cats didn't budge.

Jennifer rubbed her hand gingerly. "I'll tell you one thing, I don't feel sorry for them anymore." She shivered. "These cats are creepy."

Jamie picked up a dead branch. "I wonder if lion tamers get started this way." He poked it in front of him. "Back, you beasts! Back, I say."

The cats reluctantly retreated under his prodding. They moved slowly, hissing and whining to one another. But they were not finished yet. They surrounded the children in an angry circle.

"Can you feel that?" asked Jamie. "Boy, are they mad."

Jennifer nodded. "I think it's time we showed these cats whom they're dealing with." She opened her palm.

"Jen, you wouldn't!"

"Wouldn't what?"

"Use fireballs on them."

"Certainly not. How could you even suggest such a thing? What an insult! Just be quiet and pay attention."

A drop of water gathered in her palm. It grew larger by the second. Soon a clear ball the size of an orange was sitting there.

"It looks like a bubble," said Jamie.

"Look again," she replied. And without further ado, Jennifer threw it at the white cat.

The water ball splattered on contact. The astonished cat leaped into the air and screeched, its matted fur pressed closely around its body.

Another water ball formed in Jennifer's hand. "Who'll be next?" she asked.

None of the cats took up her challenge. They backed away, giving themselves enough distance to dodge anything thrown in their direction.

"No takers, eh?"

"True," said Jamie, "but they haven't left, either."

"Just ignore them. Our problem now is to move the can. Know any spells to make cans roll? Too bad. Neither do I. I guess we'll have to do it by hand."

They bent down to start, but no sooner was Jennifer's attention diverted than the cats moved in.

Jennifer stood up. "I can't push and keep guard at the same time. Can you manage it alone?"

Jamie tried. "Oof!" he exclaimed. "I won't be able to keep this up."

Jennifer's eyes never left the cats. She cocked her arm as one of them tensed. "Then what should we do? I'm not ready to give up."

Jamie wrinkled his nose. "Maybe we're taking

the wrong approach. We need reinforcements."

Jennifer looked around. "Who did you have in mind?"

In answer, Jamie put two fingers to his mouth and blew.

"You call that a whistle?" she said. "I didn't hear anything."

"I wasn't whistling to you. Be patient. You're not the only one in the family who practices magic, you know."

The cats were getting restless. The surprise of the water balls was wearing off, and the water itself would not inhibit them much longer. They padded warily around the children, inching closer with each revolution.

And then the first bark reached them.

The cats froze, suddenly alert. A moment later, a fox terrier reached the edge of the ridge. The cats hissed viciously. The dog just looked at Jamie and wagged its tail.

"Good dog," said Jamie. "Stay there. You're still outnumbered. We'll wait a bit."

They did not wait long. A beagle, a retriever, and two dogs that were mostly labrador soon sat on the ridge as well. They all growled at the cats below.

The cats, their ears flattened, hissed in return.

"Five cats and five dogs," Jamie counted.

"That seems fair enough. Listen carefully," he told the dogs. "These cats are not my friends or yours. What do you say to giving them a good chase?"

"Across the county, if possible," added Jennifer.

The dogs panted heavily. They were delighted to be of service.

"Ready, go!" shouted Jamie.

Whatever the cats thought of water balls, they reacted to five lunging dogs much as cats would everywhere. Like fleeting shadows, they scampered over the gully's opposite bank. The dogs followed in hot pursuit. The sound of the chase continued until the wind shifted.

"So much for the cats," said Jamie.

"Hummph!" snorted Jennifer. "You only got inspired when threatened with a little work. However," she admitted, "that whistle's a good trick."

"Thanks. Well, we'd better get going. We've still have to return the can before we head on to the library."

She nodded. "At least now I know what I'll take out today. I don't know half as much about cats as I should."

"I know what you mean," said Jamie.

SEVEN

EDWARD AND PERRY hadn't gone to the library because they had another errand to run. With Halloween just two days away, neither of them were fully prepared for the event. Despite what Jennifer might think, Perry was not above adding a distinctive touch to his pirate costume. The right detail could make a big difference, and he knew Jennifer would try awfully hard this year to outdo him. Edward was not competing with anyone, but he had been invited to a costume party, and his costume was still mostly in his head.

"A party, huh," said Perry, as they walked together. "Do you get to bring any candy home from it?"

"No," said Edward. "Whatever I eat there is all I'll get."

Perry was not impressed. "Are you sure you

wouldn't rather go out with me?" he asked.

Edward smiled. "Quite sure. I'm too old for that sort of thing."

"I hope I'm never too old. It sounds terrible."

"You will be. Wait and see."

Perry groaned. "Wait and see, wait and see. That's all I ever hear. If you're so positive I'll be going someday, tell me what these things are like."

"There's not much to tell," said Edward. "Almost everyone in my class will be there, dressed as somebody or something. We'll talk, eat, play games, and dance."

"When you say *almost everyone*, do you mean girls, too?"

"Absolutely."

"This gets worse and worse." He glanced shrewdly at Edward. "Will Carolyn be there?"

"Carolyn who?"

"I don't know. I heard Alison and Jamie talking about you and some Carolyn."

"Busybodies," fumed Edward. "You don't see me gossiping about them."

"What about the games?" Perry asked quickly, thinking it best to change the subject.

"Oh, we'll bob for apples. That's traditional. Ever done it? No? You'd like it, Perry. You have to grab a floating apple with your mouth from a wide bucket of water."

"Without your hands?"

"Right."

"Let me get this straight," said Perry. "You'll stick your head in a bucket filled with water? And people take turns doing this?" He wrinkled his nose. "You're too old for trick-or-treating but not for that, huh? I know, I know. Wait and see." He sighed. "It sure doesn't give me much to look forward to."

WESTBRIDGE did not have its own toy store, but Dickinson's Grocery stocked toys along one aisle. At this time of year, the space was largely given over to Halloween. Plastic pumpkins were heaped in a pile, waiting for fancy trick-or-treaters who didn't like to carry bags. They weren't big enough to suit Perry. Next to the pumpkins were costumes, makeup kits, wigs, and false beards, most of which came in many shapes and sizes.

Edward looked closely at the monster masks. "What a gruesome group," he said. "They seem awfully real." He put one on. "Hey, Perry, what do you think?"

"About what?"

"This mask, of course."

"What mask?"

"Very funny," Edward growled. "Boy, it's hot under here." He growled again, his hands clawing the air.

Perry watched his brother in surprise. Edward rarely made any kind of scene in public. For some reason it made Perry shudder.

"Take it off," he said suddenly.

"But why—"

"Please . . ."

The mask came off. "What's the matter?" asked Edward.

"I don't know. Your face is red."

"I said the mask was hot."

Perry nodded. Whatever had bothered him was fading away. Before he could recall it, his attention was diverted. "Wow!" he exclaimed. "Look at this!" He reached for a large rubber hook, one of several in a basket. The hook was attached to a plastic cup that fitted over the hand. "Just what I need. And it's my size, too." He took a couple of swipes through the air. "The perfect weapon for cutting my enemies to ribbons. Don't you agree?"

"Definitely," said the proprietor, Mr. Dickinson, appearing from around the corner. "Do you boys need any help?" he asked pleasantly.

"I was hoping you had a clown costume," said Edward. "You had one last year, I remember."

"So we did. Well-made and colorful, but not a big seller. This year I have a new supplier."

"We noticed a difference," Edward admitted.

Mr. Dickinson beamed. "It is a rather strong display. The salesman, Mr. Cudgel, explained to me that clowns, ballerinas, and cute animals are no longer popular. He cited a number of marketing surveys. Apparently the traditional Halloween figures have regained their original prominence. Certainly, the merchandise is of the best quality. The werewolf mask impresses me the most. It's amazing how closely synthetics can imitate the real thing. You'd think the hair on the mask was real. You may laugh, boys, but I can get a shiver just looking at it."

"I can believe it," said Perry.

Edward was disappointed. "I still miss the clowns."

"Some people have been upset, but they usually end up choosing something from what I have. These masks and costumes have a particular appeal. Sales have been very steady. You'll be seeing all kinds of demons, monsters, zombies, werewolves, and vampires this Halloween." He chuckled. "I'm glad I'm not going out."

"They don't scare me," Perry insisted. "I've matched my wits with many a scurvy foe."

Mr. Dickinson smiled. "From the cut of your jib, I'd say you were a rather fierce pirate." He stroked his chin. "Have you seen the collection of scars, running sores, and open wounds down at the other end? Every pirate should have at least one reminder of an earlier battle."

Perry raised his hook sternly. "It is bad enough that I lost my hand to a shark and an eye to a misfiring. But do not insult my fighting ability. No blade or bullet has ever struck me."

Edward nudged him. "You'll have to excuse Perry, Mr. Dickinson. Sometimes he gets carried away."

"Quite all right. Used to do the same thing myself. My apologies, Captain."

Perry bowed.

Mr. Dickinson turned back to Edward. "What about yourself? See anything that catches your fancy?"

Edward sighed. He shook away the temptation to change his mind. "I'm not really in a zombie mood. I wanted to be a clown. I guess I'll just get a makeup kit and figure out the rest later."

"All right. Come up to the register when you're ready."

"Thanks, Mr. Dickinson." Edward found himself staring again at the monster masks while Perry clawed the air with the hook. What about them was so troubling? Masks were only masks, weren't they? Yet most of the ones he had seen before had exaggerated or goofy features. They were as likely to make people laugh as scream. But these masks were not funny. They were grim. Everything was drawn or molded in gruesome detail.

"Edward?"

"Hmmmmm. . . ."

A rubber hook slid around his throat. He slipped free of it with a start.

"I thought that would get your attention," said Perry. "You're lucky I didn't slit your throat. I rarely show mercy. Are you ready to go?"

"I suppose so." He picked up a deluxe makeup kit, stuck out his tongue at the rows of masks, and followed Perry up the aisle.

He did not look back.

EIGHT

I THINK DINNER went off smoothly," said Amelia Harding, opening the door to her mother's room.

Madeleine Harding grunted. "What was that they served us?" she asked.

"Creamed chicken."

I must remember to include it in my next brew. It had a properly disagreeable smell." She grimaced at her canopied bed and patchwork quilt coverlet. "Are you sure I have to stay here, Amelia?"

"Mother, we went through this already. I am sorry, but every room here is bright, clean, and cheery. There's nothing I can do about it. And this inn is the only place to stay in Westbridge. Alison told me the management is very proud of the decor."

Mrs. Harding folded her arms. "How little

they know. Speaking of Alison, where has that girl gone to?"

"I sent her home."

"I'm glad you're finally showing some sense. Why did you ever have her sit with us through lunch and dinner? It hardly allowed for any proper conversation."

"How much could we have discussed with the waiters hovering nearby? Besides, you saw how proud she looked. Imagine her dismay when she discovers that she helped in our plan."

"Yes," her mother admitted, "that will be nice."

There was a knock at the door.

"Enter, Cudgel." Mrs. Harding looked around as the door opened. "Where has Agatha gone to?"

Cudgel cleared his throat. "The cat adjourned to the garden, Madam. She seemed fatigued, and her fur was covered with brambles. I suspect she was involved in some kind of chase. The other cats look much the same."

Madeleine nodded. "Already having some fun, no doubt." She ran her finger along the edge of the mantle. "This is disgusting. Not a hint of dust. Cudgel, return to the garden and bring back some dirt. If I must stay here, I may as well be comfortable."

"Mother," said Amelia, "the rooms are cleaned every day."

"So? Go, Cudgel."

He left the room.

Amelia sighed. "Very well, Mother. But why jeopardize the plan by needlessly—"

"Silence! I will take responsibility for the matter." She settled herself in a chair. "Now, what do you have to report?"

"Everyone is very curious, of course. That's to be expected."

Madeleine Harding allowed herself a smile. "It will do them good to show some patience. I was patient for years while searching among ancient books and manuscripts."

"Will you reveal the whole plan tonight?"

"I will tell the participants what they need to know. Just as I have with you and Cudgel. Have you had any other problems?"

Amelia shook her head. "The only real issue was where to keep the perishable supplies. I ended up refrigerating them in the restaurant kitchen. They're in opaque jars, and the lids are sealed with a closing spell. I made it clear to the cook that the jars should not be disturbed."

"Then we are set to begin. We have taken every precaution. No one is going to spoil this for me."

Amelia went to the door. "I'll escort you to the meeting in an hour. Meanwhile you should get some rest."

"I am not a child, Amelia. I will rest when I see fit."

"As you wish, Mother," she said slowly, and shut the door behind her.

GREAT BEAMS stretched across the ceiling of the meeting room assigned to the Harding conference. Tall windows filled with small panes were spaced along the outer wall, though at present they were covered with crimson drapes. A fire burned in the fieldstone fireplace at one end, the only light to be seen.

Madeleine Harding stood watching the burning logs while Amelia greeted the conference members. Once they were seated, Madeleine turned to observe her audience. Some of the faces were familiar; others she had not seen before. But bitterness, greed, and ambition had left their marks on them all. She was pleased. They would make worthy accomplices.

Amelia stood at a podium. "Good evening," she said. "I welcome you to our first official gathering. Some of you are sitting among friends. Some know one another solely by reputation. We all share, however, one thing in common—our pursuit of witchcraft. It is to further that pursuit that we have come here." She paused. "We have much to accomplish tonight. But before we begin, everyone must submit to a binding spell."

A disapproving murmur filled the room.

Nathaniel Mandrake rose from his seat. "In all my years of practicing the Black Arts, I have never permitted such a thing. I do not propose to begin now."

"Well put!"

"My thoughts exactly."

"Do not be hasty," said Sarah MacGregor, her needles clicking diligently. "Let's not unravel the conference at the start. I am no more accustomed to binding spells than the rest of you. Yet surely the Hardings anticipated our reluctance. Hence, I assume they have a good reason for asking. I suggest we at least hear them out."

"Thank you, Sarah," Amelia continued. "I appreciate your forebearance. It is not really my place to explain further. My mother is the force behind this conference. She will answer your questions."

The participants clapped politely.

Madeleine Harding straightened her back as she emerged from the shadows. She stared grimly at her peers. "You have come here blindly at my bidding," she began. "None of you need fear that I will disappoint that trust. We are gathered in Westbridge to settle a score. It is a score too long neglected. In the modern world, science has supplanted magic. And as magic has been eclipsed, so have we. Our deeds are now consigned to the darkness, to things and events of lesser importance. Witches and warlocks are no longer the advisors of kings and queens. Indeed, for most people they exist only in foolish fairy tales. Even those of us who wield some power lack the scope of our ancestors. I have a plan to change that. I will share it with you, but the binding spell must come first. It will serve both as a sensible precaution against betrayal and as a symbol of our dedication to a common goal."

"And what is that goal?" asked Jocelyn Grant.

"First, the binding spell," replied Madeleine. "We begin there or not at all."

The participants looked around uneasily, taking the measure of one another. Madeleine Harding had prodded their discontent, yet that feeling also fostered a sense of mistrust and suspicion.

Amelia noted their indecision. "Surely," she said, "we would not ask you this over some trifling matter. Remember, the spell will only ensure us a level of secrecy. You cannot be forced to do anything against your will."

"Are there still any objections?" Madeleine asked.

Many glances were exchanged, but nobody spoke.

"Excellent," she continued. "I assure you that your faith will be amply rewarded. Please rise now and form a circle around me."

The circle was quickly made. Amelia stood directly in front of her mother. The others spaced themselves around the room. "I will start," said Amelia, speaking in a clear voice:

> *I begin the spell*
> *By pledging my word*
> *That what I learn here*
> *Will never be heard*
> *By anyone else*
> *Who if told of our plot*
> *Might try to undo*
> *The work that we wrought.*

Sarah MacGregor was standing to her right, and she took up the next verse.

> *This spell I strengthen*
> *By giving my trust*

To those gathered here
Who in return must
Give theirs back to me
While the magic is cast
Where it shall be held
Till its purpose is past.

This verse was repeated with slight variations by everyone present. When they were done, Madeleine raised her arms and said:

Thirteen are thus bound
It is now known by all
When the Witching Hour ends
So too will end this call.

The air above their head glowed red, leaving behind a bitter smell. With the ceremony completed, the participants returned to their seats.

"We have indulged you, Madeleine," said Max Gunther. "Now you must indulge us. What scheme have you devised for us?"

"Always so direct, Max. Very well. First, I will explain why we are meeting in this sleepy village. It is a source of the Old Magic. Whether the Old Magic is in a person, an object, or the land itself I do not know. Nor do I have any way of finding out."

"Then of what use is this discovery?" asked Phoebe Tokla.

"Patience," Madeleine said sharply. "I propose that we make the Old Magic find us. As you know, the Old Magic is not learned. In a person it is inherited; in an object or the land it simply exists. But because of its nature, it can be drawn upon. Imagine what we could accomplish working together with its aid."

Her audience had a vivid imagination. Scenes of terror and destruction swarmed in everyone's head.

"The incantation is complicated," Madeleine continued. "Are there any objections to attempting it tonight? Good. I see we are now in harmony. Observe the brass lantern hanging overhead. It is there we will capture and hold the Old Magic. Sarah and Nathaniel, you will assist me directly. The rest of you will follow Amelia's instructions."

It took more than an hour for the room to be prepared. Dozens of black candles were lit and arranged along the walls. They burned with a red light, emitting the smell of a swamp in summer. The rising vapor swirled above a floor covered by signs and arcane symbols. Largest of all was the pentagram drawn in the center.

Madeleine Harding had spent the time explaining the procedure to her two helpers. Now she leaned heavily against the podium, conserving her strength for the task ahead.

"Are you ready, Mother?" Amelia asked. Her hands were smudged with chalk from her work on the floor.

"I am prepared," Madeleine answered, taking her place in the middle of the pentagram.

The others took up positions around her. Sarah MacGregor and Nathaniel Mandrake stood to her left and right. One witch stood on each of the pentagram's five points, and the remaining five, including Amelia, formed an outer circle.

"We begin," Madeleine intoned darkly. Her expression grew suddenly blank. Drops of perspiration lined her brow. In a cold and stony voice, she said:

We search for the Old Magic,
Wherever it lies,
To make it our own,
To break its past ties.

Both Sarah and Nathaniel now pressed their hands together. Slowly, their fingers started to glow. The points of the pentagram glowed as well. The witches above them went stiff, feeding their support to Madeleine. The five outer members walked around them, chanting dirges in a low chorus.

After a time, Madeleine raised her head. The lantern was dark. She clenched her fists and spoke again.

> *Out farther and farther,*
> *The search must go on,*
> *The task undertaken,*
> *Till our last strength is gone.*

Faster and faster the chanters circled the pentagram, their words and movements blurring together. The candles' flames lengthened, and rivulets of black wax dripped down their sides.

But the lantern remained dark.

Madeleine Harding trembled. Even their combined efforts had not demonstrated the proper strength. "I must take a greater chance," she thought. Humming to herself, she began rocking back and forth. With each swing she faded slightly, like a shadow when a cloud passes before the sun.

Her companions recognized the risk she was taking. Madeleine had added her life force to the spell. It was a mighty aid, but if she faded away completely before the spell was done, she would simply be gone. Forever. Should the spell be successful, she would recover her form.

The candle flames rose higher and higher. The mists churned in curling eddies. And then without warning, the candles blinked out. But the room was not dark.

The lantern had begun to glow.

NINE

FOR THE THIRD TIME," said Jennifer, "I don't care how strange it sounds. That's what happened."

Edward grinned.

"If you had been there," said Jamie, "you wouldn't think it was funny. I'm sure Perry believes us."

Perry was admiring his hook. "So you met some hungry cats. Big deal."

"Oh?" Jennifer was getting mad. "How many hungry cats do you know that will roll a milk can hundreds of yards? Not to mention defending that can against magic water balls."

"I give up," said Perry. "How many?"

"This is serious," insisted Jamie. "Those were not ordinary cats."

"No?" said Edward. "What kind were they?"

"We're not positive," Jamie admitted. "But

we did some research at the library. Did you know that the ancient Egyptians worshipped cats?"

Perry yawned.

"Is that important?" asked Edward.

"Of course," said Jennifer. "It shows that cats are special. And that's not all. They're also the most common form of familiar."

"Familiar what?" asked Perry.

"Just *familiar*. Period. A familiar is an animal that has an unusual relationship with a witch. Some sort of companion."

"That's nice," said Edward. "We wouldn't want witches to be lonely."

"You're so thick," said Jamie. "Don't you see? If these cats are familiars, then there must be witches nearby."

"That's a big *if*," Edward noted.

"Real witches?" said Perry.

Jennifer nodded. "Those cats were spooky."

"How could witches live in Westbridge without our knowing it? You'd think our paths would have crossed by now."

Jamie sighed. "We thought of that, too. It just makes things more mysterious."

The front door banged open.

"Hello!" shouted Alison. "Anyone home?"

"We're in the study," Edward called out.

"Ah," she said, poking her head through the doorway. "A gathering of the clan."

"You're home early," said Jamie.

"Miss Harding had no need for me at the meeting tonight, so she sent me home."

"And what did you learn about the conference?" asked Edward.

Alison smiled weakly. "Actually, not much. The people seem nice enough, a little old-fashioned. But they didn't talk about the subject of the conference all day." She shrugged. "I guess I'll find out tomorrow. Anyway, you should hear what happened this morning. Miss Harding and I were outside, waiting for her mother to arrive, when the assistant manager came strutting out. He was upset because some of the conference members brought their cats with them."

"Cats!" exclaimed Jamie and Jennifer.

"That's right," said Alison in surprise. "Cats."

"Go on, go on," said Jennifer.

"The assistant manager told Miss Harding that pets are not allowed in the rooms. And he said it in this stuffy voice. But did Miss Harding cringe under his attack?"

"We don't know," said Perry. "You're telling the story."

75

Alison frowned at him. "Just listen. With scarcely a pause for breath, she parried all his complaints. You should've seen him. He deflated like a punctured balloon."

"What about the cats?" asked Jamie.

"Well, now they get to stay, of course. But that's not the important thing. It was the way Miss Harding handled the situation that mattered."

"But did you see them?" Jennifer said excitedly.

"The cats? Only two. What difference does it make?"

"What color were they?" Jamie asked.

"One was white, the other black."

"Friendly?" asked Jennifer.

"Not exactly. Say, what's going on?"

"Jennifer and Jamie are looking for familiars," Perry explained.

"Familiars? You mean like witches' familiars? That's ridiculous."

"No, it's not," said Jamie. "Jen and I came across some strange cats this afternoon. They had stolen a milk can, and they weren't afraid of us or our magic."

"And now," added Jennifer, "you tell us there are strangers with cats in town. And two of the cats we saw were black and white, too."

"You call that evidence?" said Alison. "You think they're the only black and white cats in Massachusetts? Anyway, the whole idea is silly. These people can't be witches. I ate lunch and dinner with them." She grinned ruefully. "We all suffered together through the creamed chicken. Surely witches wouldn't put up with that. I know Perry wouldn't."

"I would in public," Perry insisted.

"But . . ." Jennifer began.

Alison shook her head. "Don't bother elaborating. I'm not interested. This conference is not mysterious. It's being held out in the open."

"Perhaps that's the best way to avoid attention," said Jamie.

Alison snorted.

"The conference may not be mysterious," said Edward, "but it's still a mystery to you."

"I have heard enough," Alison said firmly. "More than enough, in fact. It's been a long day, and I'm tired. I have to get up early tomorrow. Since you're so suspicious, I'll tell you what's on the schedule. First, there's breakfast. Lots of sinister eggs, toast, and cereal. Then a tour of the town. After a diabolical lunch of soup and sandwiches, a nature walk is planned. Satisfied? Good night!"

She turned abruptly and marched upstairs.

The others just looked at one another.

"You won't get much support from her," Edward remarked.

"Maybe not," said Jennifer, "but that doesn't change anything. Those cats deserve further investigation."

Perry yawned again.

"Perhaps we should ask Father's advice," suggested Jamie. "He may know how to tell familiars apart from regular animals."

"You can't ask him now," said Edward. "He and Mother went to a faculty party. You'll have to wait till they come home."

HEADLIGHTS SWEPT across the house as a car pulled into the Wynd's driveway. Like soldiers mustering for inspection, Edward, Jamie, and Jennifer stood by the front door, waiting for their parents to come in. Perry had already gone to bed.

Three minutes passed.

"They're taking a long time," Jamie commented.

Jennifer looked out the window. "Oh!" she gasped. "Something's wrong. Father isn't walking well."

No one waited to hear any more. They rushed outside.

"What happened?"

"Did you have an accident?"

"Are you all right, Father?"

Professor Wynd greeted them with a grin. "I'm fine, just fine." Then he stumbled. "Well, maybe a little tired."

"It could be the flu," said Elizabeth, searching her husband's face intently. "Or simply too many hors d'oeuvres."

"I only had a few," he protested weakly.

"A few too many, you mean. But let's not stand here in the cold. Edward, run upstairs and turn down the bed. Jennifer, start some water boiling for tea. Jamie, you can take my place under your father's shoulder."

With their combined help, the professor was soon settled comfortably in bed. Jamie pulled the curtains closed while Edward puffed up the pillows.

"I appreciate your concern," said their father, as Jennifer appeared with the tea. "But there's no need to be worried. I just got a little dizzy when we passed through town. Nothing too serious." He took a sip of tea. "I'm going to follow your mother's advice and get a good night's sleep."

"It's about time you started listening to me," she said. "All right, children, out you go. I'll see you off to bed." She ushered them into the hall and shut the door.

Professor Wynd stretched out under the blankets. "Ridiculous," he muttered, "getting sick at my age. I'm too old for such nonsense." He rolled over on his side. "I do feel odd, though. Incomplete, somehow." His eyelids grew heavy.

"Shouldn't leave the light on," he murmured. But he was too tired to sit up. So he conjured a spell to flick the switch.

But when Elizabeth returned a few minutes later, the lamp was still on.

TEN

WESTBRIDGE CENTER was usually a quiet place on Sundays. And that Sunday was no different, except on the side steps of the library.

"I'm still not sure why I came," said Edward. He stretched his arms and yawned.

"Because," replied Jamie, "you'd hate to find out later we were right."

"Maybe. But I'm certainly not going to find out sitting here."

"We're not just sitting," said Jennifer. "We're staking out the inn. Father is too sick for us to bother him with questions. We have to investigate on our own."

"Couldn't we investigate from the green?" asked Perry. "It's more comfortable there. And none of these conference people know us."

"True," said Jamie, "but Alison does. And

she'd have a fit if she knew we were here."

"She wouldn't like it," Perry admitted. "But how long do we have to wait?"

Jamie shrugged. "Lunch should be over soon. When they leave on their nature walk, we'll follow them. Meanwhile, we wait."

Jennifer leaned her head against her hand. "Right," she said.

Edward peered over the railing. "They're coming," he announced.

Several people were emerging from the inn's front entrance, Alison among them. She stood on the porch, talking to a tall woman.

"Maybe that's Miss Harding," said Jamie.

Edward sighed. "She doesn't look too menacing from here."

Perry looked disappointed. "How can they be witches?" he asked. "I don't see any pointed hats."

"Of course not," said Jennifer. "They're trying to be inconspicuous. They're here in secret, remember?"

"In disguise, eh?" said Perry. "Pretty clever."

"It's only clever if they're actually witches," Edward reminded them. "We haven't exactly proven that yet."

"We will," said Jennifer.

"So now what?" asked Perry.

"We stick to the plan," said Jamie. "Keep a good watch for anything suspicious."

"What about Alison?" asked Edward.

"She just went back inside," said Jennifer. "And I know that walk of hers. She isn't happy. I'll bet she's not going."

"She may have work to do," guessed Jamie. "All the better for us."

Edward stood up. "Let's get going," he said. "We don't want to lose them."

For the next hour, at least, there was little chance of that. The conference members ambled along the road like any group out for a stroll. Some of them carried spades and others shouldered burlap bags, which made them look about as suspicious as a garden club. They made frequent stops, filling the bags with whatever they dug up.

The Wynds observed all this from the woods.

"I feel silly," said Edward, his doubts reasserting themselves.

"They're sneaky," Jennifer admitted. "Trying to act normal to put people off their track."

"What if they're not acting, Jen?" Edward asked.

She frowned.

"I haven't even seen any cats," muttered Perry. He'd been looking forward to it.

"Just a bit longer," said Jamie. "We can. . . . Oh, oh. They're splitting up."

The conference members had parted into two distinct groups, moving in opposite directions.

"Do we go home now?" asked Perry.

"Yes," said Edward.

"No," said Jennifer. "We'll split up, too. Jamie, you and I can take one skeptic apiece."

Jamie nodded. "Come on, Perry," he said. "We'll take the ones heading down the slope."

Jennifer and Edward followed the rest. Most of them continued digging in a nearby glen. One woman, though, wandered over to the road and a small farm stand. The two children watched her from behind a stone wall.

"What's she doing?" Jennifer wondered.

Edward shrugged. "Maybe she's hungry."

The woman stooped only briefly and then returned to the glen.

"Should we investigate?" asked Jennifer.

"Investigate what?" said Edward.

"You know. What we just saw."

"Is that worth investigating?"

"It's a start."

Edward grinned. "Lead on, Sherlock."

They approached the farm stand casually, as though they had just happened along. Jennifer even whistled a little, much to Edward's embarrassment. He thought she was overdoing it.

Behind the counter sat Charlie Fisher, who had known the children all their lives. He saw them coming. "Well, look what the wind blew in," he called out. Then he laughed. Charlie always enjoyed his own jokes.

"Hi, Mr. Fisher," they said together.

"I understand you did me a service yesterday, Jennifer. I don't know how that milk can got away, but I appreciate your returning it. They're hard to replace."

"We were glad to help."

Charlie nodded. "My, you two get bigger every time we meet. The world's certainly a changing place." He looked up and down the road. "Of course," he added, "not much is changing in my particular corner of it. I haven't sold a pumpkin for. . . . Are you feeling all right, Jennifer? You look sort of pale."

She was pale. Edward had blanched a bit, too. They had both noticed the pumpkins sitting in rows behind Mr. Fisher. Each one had a hideous grin carved on its face. The children knew better than to think that Charlie Fisher sold them that way.

"Hasn't anyone been by?" Edward asked.

"Just a young woman a few minutes ago. She was a strange sort, thought my pumpkins could

use some improvement." He snorted. "I grow the finest pumpkins in these parts. And I told her so. She mumbled something back that I didn't catch. Then she giggled and left."

"Your pumpkins always have been the best," Edward agreed. "And they should stay that way. Right, Jen?"

She nodded.

Charlie beamed. "I appreciate the compliment. I suppose she was entitled to her opinion. I mean, it takes all kinds. . . . Say, what are you two staring at?"

He turned around. For a moment, he could have sworn his pumpkins all looked like jack o'lanterns. He blinked in surprise, and the pumpkins were as plump and orange as ever.

"We were admiring your pumpkins," Edward said smoothly.

Jennifer smiled. "I'm sure they'll make fine jack o'lanterns."

Charlie rubbed his eyes. "Did you kids see . . . Aw, forget it. Remind me to stay out of the sun."

"Well, we should be going," said Edward.

"Goodbye," added Jennifer.

Charlie watched them go. "Nice kids," he murmured, "but they look worried. They should get more rest." He remembered the pumpkins. "So should I." Having said that, he closed his eyes and took a little nap.

JAMIE AND PERRY had shadowed their quarry for a half hour with nothing to show for it. Perry had been discouraged from the start, and even Jamie was losing his enthusiasm.

"All they do," he said, "is walk along, bend down, pull up plants and put them in their sacks."

Perry kicked a stone. "Maybe Alison was right."

"We could try to get closer," Jamie suggested. "They could be saying things we should hear."

Perry liked that. It sounded dangerous.

Creeping forward on their hands and knees, the two brothers closed the gap between themselves and their prey. The tall grass hid their movements from any watchful eyes.

"Look near the moss," someone said.

"The poisonous ones are flatter," added another voice.

Perry squirmed uncomfortably in his hiding place. A rock was nudging him in the ribs.

"Keep still," hissed Jamie.

"This will be splendid," a woman called out. "Fully up to the Black Forest's standards. Take a look."

Perry started to raise his head.

Jamie pulled him down. "What are you doing?" he whispered.

"I want to see what she found."

Jamie thought it over. It might be their first lead. "Make it quick," he said.

Perry lifted his head. He pulled it down again fast, like a turtle retreating into its shell.

"Well?"

"A man was staring this way."

"Did he see you?"

Perry shook his head.

"Are you —"

The swishing sound of legs wading through the nearby grass was unmistakable.

"Don't bother over there, Nathaniel. Nothing we need grows in the grasses."

"No?" The swishing stopped.

Jamie and Perry held their breaths.

"Very well." The man laughed, and the swishing retreated.

Several minutes passed before the children relaxed.

"I think they're gone," said Jamie. "It should be safe to get up."

Perry stood up and promptly fell down.

Jamie smothered a laugh. But when he stood up, the same thing happened.

"My feet feel like lead," said Perry. "They won't budge. How can we follow anyone now?"

"Maybe that was the idea." Jamie smiled. "At least we got some proof of magic."

Perry eyed his feet as if they had betrayed him. "Can we do anything about this?"

Jamie sighed. "I don't know any spells to lighten my feet. If we're lucky, it'll wear off soon."

They propped themselves up as comfortably as possible and waited.

ELEVEN

A S ALISON went back inside the inn, she could feel the frustration rising within her. How could she not be included on a nature walk? Wasn't she the most likely guide for any tours of the area? Obviously Miss Harding thought otherwise. She had even joked about setting off flares if they got lost. Of course, it was true that Alison had errands to perform in their absence. Still, that didn't make her feel any better.

"Urrgh," she grumbled, crossing the lobby. None of this would have mattered if Jamie and Jennifer had not voiced their suspicions the night before. Now she was questioning everything in spite of herself. The cats were rather unfriendly, but so what? Why did other people's suspicions make a difference when you thought you didn't believe them? Why couldn't she just forget about it and concentrate on her job? But it wasn't that easy. The whole issue was like an itch she couldn't quite reach. And it refused to go away.

"Alison?"

The manager of the inn was calling to her.

"Yes?"

"Could I see you for a minute? We haven't spoken much, I realize. I've been busy since I returned from Boston. Do you know where Miss Harding is? I'd like to ask her a question."

"She's gone out, probably for the whole afternoon."

"Hmmmm. . . . Perhaps you can help me. Miss Harding requested a roaring fire at tonight's meeting, but I don't know what time it will start. It's hard to make fires roar without sufficient warning. Do you know when the meeting will begin?"

Alison shook her head. "I could go get a schedule. It may be written there."

"No, no, I have one right here." He tapped a sheet of paper on his desk. "All it says is *Sunday night: Meeting.* That's not too specific. In fact, the entire schedule is rather vague. Receptions, luncheons, dinners, meetings—that's all anyone knows about this conference. Most schedules list the titles of the sessions, the names of speakers, and other things." He laughed. "You'd almost think they had something to hide. Would I be prying to ask what's going on?"

Alison blushed. "I really don't know, either." It was starting to bother her more than she wanted to admit.

"Don't mistake me," the manager added hastily. "I'm not being critical. I have no complaint with the Hardings. Few people pay in advance these days." He paused. "If you don't mind, I'd appreciate your keeping this conversation between us. No need to ruffle any feathers."

"I understand," said Alison. "I've been curious, too. If I find out anything, I'll let you know."

"Excellent. You've been doing a fine job, Alison. It wouldn't surprise me if we hired you ourselves to work at future conferences."

"Thank you." She smiled. "Is there anything else? I have to go check on the supplies for the cocktail party."

"No, go ahead. And remember, mum's the word."

The inn's kitchen served the Different Drummer Restaurant as well as room service and special functions in places like the Ethan Allen Room. All three types of meals were presided over by Bill Smathers, the cook on duty.

"What can I do for you, today?" he asked Alison, as she came through the swinging door.

"Nothing, Mr. Smathers. I'm checking on the stuff we'll be using later. Do you know where it is?"

He pointed with a knife toward a large refrigerator. "In there," he said. "On the left-hand side. The cheese is in the door, and the trays are on the bottom shelf."

Alison opened the refrigerator. Everything was in its proper place. "What about the crackers?" she asked.

"In the cabinet," he replied. "I'm glad you'll be taking those trays out. I can use the space. Any idea when you'll be needing the three jars on the top shelf?"

"I'm afraid not."

Mr. Smathers sighed and began washing a pot.

Alison pulled down one of the jars. Miss Harding had made no mention of them. Were they important? On the lid was written: "Harding Conference—DO NOT OPEN." Alison hesitated. So many mysteries surrounded this conference. Surely this was one she could solve. The DO NOT OPEN was undoubtedly meant for inn employees. It would not apply to her. Besides, the jars might hold something she would want for the reception.

Alison tried to unscrew the lid. She kept at it

until her fingers ached. The lid wouldn't turn. "So much for muscle," she muttered. Tracing her finger around the seal of the jar, she murmured a spell. The lid should then have twisted off by itself.

It didn't.

Alison frowned. That spell always worked on the pickle jars at home. The lid was just being stubborn. Well, she could be stubborn, too. She repeated the spell, this time tracing her whole hand around the seal.

The jar trembled in her hands. Alison feared it would shatter, but slowly the lid began turning. Then it stopped and reversed direction. The lid spun back and forth like a confused propeller. She put her hand over it lightly. The next time the lid began to turn off, she added her strength to the effort.

The lid popped into her hand.

Bill Smathers looked up suddenly and shut off the water. "Did you just scream?" he asked.

Alison shook her head.

"Sorry. I sometimes hear things with the water running."

Alison smiled weakly and turned away. She couldn't trust her face to any further scrutiny from the cook. There was no reason to involve him, even though she *had* screamed. Anyone might have screamed, she told herself. Steeling her resolve, she glanced again at the open jar.

It was filled with dead lizards.

Alison swallowed hard, replaced the lid, and returned the jar to the shelf. She felt better at once. Her thoughts were all jumbled, though. What did lizards have to do with the conference? Were they some kind of joke?

"Mr. Smathers?"

The cook shut off the water again.

"Who brought these jars in here?"

"Miss Harding did. She said they were perishable delicacies. I remember because she laughed when I asked if they needed any special preparation. All she wanted, she said, was the space in the refrigerator." He frowned. "Is anything wrong? I haven't touched the jars. And they're labeled, of course."

"No, no, they're fine. I was just wondering."

He nodded and resumed his work.

Alison eyed the two remaining jars. What secrets did they hold? She didn't want another shock, but she was curious. And no one was watching. . . .

The second lid gave her as much trouble as the first. She was prepared now, however, and soon had it off. The contents were not heart-stopping, just some brown powder mixed with some kind of kernels. The third jar was more what she expected. Whatever that jellylike substance was, it looked disgusting and smelled worse. Alison wasn't sure what to think of these *delicacies*. For the moment, she simply returned the jars to the shelf.

"Having any trouble, Miss Wynd?"

Alison whirled around. Nicholas Cudgel was standing by the kitchen door. "You startled me, Mr. Cudgel. I thought you had gone with the others."

"You were mistaken," he said brusquely. "Mrs. Harding left me with some instructions."

"I see."

"She thought you might need help preparing for the reception. I am here to assist you."

Cudgel had given no sign that anything was amiss, but Alison still felt uneasy. "That's nice of you," she said. "I was just checking on the refreshments."

Cudgel made a brief nod. "And what have you found?"

"We have several kinds of cheese and three trays of hors d'oeuvres."

"And the crackers?"

Alison opened the cabinet. Boxes of crackers were lined up neatly in rows.

"I am glad everything is in order. I believe you

can now shut the refrigerator door. You are finished in there?"

Alison closed it at once. "I haven't put out the glasses yet," she added. "Maybe I should do that next."

"Maybe you should," he agreed, stepping aside to let her pass.

" 'Bye, Mr. Smathers," Alison said quickly. She did not wait for him to look up.

"Nice girl," the cook remarked.

Cudgel grimaced. "Yes," he said, "I'm afraid she is."

THE TINKLE of wine glasses surrounded Alison as she walked among the conference members serving hors d'oeuvres. She wasn't paying much attention to them. Her mind was preoccupied with dead lizards. Why did the Hardings need them? Jennifer would have said that witches have lots of uses for such things. But these people didn't look like witches.

Alison smiled a bit ruefully. What did she know about how witches would look? She was tempted to ask Miss Harding outright about the jars. Yet if the worse were true, that would be stupid and dangerous. There, she was making assumptions again. Still, those horrid-smelling burlap sacks the participants had returned with were hardly reassuring. Miss Harding had made some quick mention of "souvenirs." But for what purpose would anyone collect such things?

"Is anything wrong?" asked Miss Harding, tapping her on the shoulder.

Alison looked embarrassed. "I was daydreaming, I guess. I'm sorry."

Under Miss Harding's watchful gaze, Alison continued circulating through the room. She appeared oblivious to the swirls of conversation around her, but she was listening to every word.

". . . I haven't the faintest idea what she has in mind. The Old — Yes, thank you. I'll have a cheese-filled one."

". . . I gave a couple of snoopy kids something to think about. It's a variation of the Welsh millstone method. Makes the feet—No, no, I'm watching my weight."

". . . And to think Halloween is tomorrow night. If I see even one of those horrid masks with the warts and dangling nose, I'll— Don't take that kind. Try the cracker with the little fish that stares at you. What's that called?"

"An anchovy, I think," said Alison.

She raised her glass. "Cheers."

Alison replenished the tray several times. The only fact she discovered was that a few people can eat a lot of hors d'oeuvres. As for what she had heard, she was no less puzzled than before. She had noticed, though, that the subject of conversation abruptly changed in her presence. Alison had the uneasy feeling she held pieces of a jigsaw puzzle without any guide as to what the final picture should be.

When the participants finally began returning to their rooms, Miss Harding approached her again. "You've been very industrious this past hour," she said. "And most attentive. Once the reception is over, you'll be free to leave."

"But surely after dinner. . . ."

Miss Harding smiled tightly. "Your dedication is admirable, but dinner will be followed by another meeting. You can't help there."

"I am interested, though. If I could sit—"

"That would be impossible." Miss Harding tapped her chin. "You see, Alison, some of the participants would hesitate to speak in your presence. Some of the matters we discuss are personal."

"Oh."

"Have no fear, I'll have plenty for you to do tomorrow. Now you must excuse me. My mother is expecting me upstairs."

Alison helped clean up and then got her coat. She didn't meet anyone on her way out, which was just as well. She had a lot to think about.

TWELVE

JENNIFER was pacing up and down the hall with enormous precision. "Where are they?" she muttered, her hands clasped firmly behind her back.

Edward's head swung back and forth following her movements. "You know, Jennifer, if someone put you in a clock, you'd probably keep good time. But you shouldn't let yourself get so worked up."

"We've been home for an hour."

"That's true. But we didn't say when we'd meet Jamie and Perry or even where. They could be looking for us."

Jennifer grunted. "It wouldn't be fair if they got to do something exciting. But is that likely? Just wait till I tell Perry what happened to those pumpkins. That'll teach him not to be skeptical."

"I was skeptical, too," Edward reminded her. He peered out the window. "Here they come now. By the look of them I'd say nothing much exciting happened. They're really dragging their heels."

Jennifer opened the door. "Come on, slow-pokes!" she shouted.

Jamie waved at her. "Well, they've seen us," he said.

"Good." Perry sat down. "This is close enough. Let them come to us."

Jamie needed no persuading. He plopped wearily to the ground.

Edward and Jennifer shared a frown between them. What was going on? They grabbed their coats and ran outside.

"What's the matter?" Edward asked, reaching his brothers' side.

Perry sighed. "I feel as if I'm wearing lead shoes."

"Me, too," said Jamie. "But they're getting lighter. The spell is wearing off."

"Spell?" repeated Jennifer.

Jamie nodded. "That's right. At least one of those conference members can do magic."

"Make that two," said Edward. He told them about the jack o'lanterns.

Perry whistled. "Poor Mr. Fisher. He must

think he's going crazy."

"He did look confused," said Jennifer.

"Has Father gotten over what's bothering him?" Jamie asked.

"Well, he's not any worse."

"And no better, either," said Edward. "He doesn't feel sick, he said, just weak. As if a part of him is missing."

Jamie shook his head. "It's strange. We'll go in to see him when our feet get back to normal. We shouldn't mention any of this witch business, though. It would only worry him."

"But we should tell Mother," said Jennifer.

"True," agreed Edward. "Yet the first person to tell is Alison. We can't go talking about those people behind her back, and we'll need her help to do a proper investigation."

"It might not be as bad as we think," said Jamie. "Maybe the witches are only having some kind of annual meeting."

"Possible," Jennifer admitted, "but not very likely. Why would they gather plants and roots for a meeting?"

There was no easy answer to that.

WHILE THE OTHERS waited for Alison's return by working on their Halloween costumes, Perry decided to have a dress rehearsal. He put on the patched rags he saved from year to year, tied a red kerchief around his forehead, and placed a black patch over his right eye. After adding smudges of mascara on his cheeks he was just about ready.

The final touch was the hook. He removed it from a drawer and admired it at arm's length. The hook looked more like cold steel than painted rubber. Perry slid it over his left hand. "Take that, you landlubber," he sneered. It was easy to imagine his foe falling back in terror.

Perry swaggered across the rug, gazing at himself in the dresser mirror. A hook was a useful thing, he thought, good for climbing trees and scratching his back. Perry adjusted the laces. This particular hook fit snugly over his hand. What spell would it take to change it into a real hook? Perry sighed. He had no way of knowing. Still, an illusion was better than nothing. If he could make squash look like pudding . . .

Perry uttered a spell similar to the one he had said two nights before at dinner. The transformation came quickly. Too quickly. The hook gleamed with the sparkle of the finest Damascus steel.

Perry winced.

More than the hook had been affected. His wrist ached horribly. Then the ache began to

burn. Perry thrashed about, scraping the hook against the bedpost. Desperately, he pulled at it. The hook remained bound to his wrist.

At that moment he screamed.

Seconds later, his mother rushed into the room. "What's wrong?" she cried.

Perry ran to her at once. The pain stopped as he was caught in her embrace, like a light that had been switched off. "Oh!" he gasped, the tears streaming down his face.

Mrs. Wynd held him close. She had never seen him so upset before. "Are you all right now?" she asked gently. "Can you tell me what happened?"

Perry stepped back. He blinked several times and wiped away his tears. The pain had completely vanished. He tugged again at the hook. It came off easily.

"Perry?"

He smiled sheepishly. "I screamed, didn't I?"

She nodded.

"My wrist hurt. I was trying to make my hook look real. And I did. Then the pain . . . and the hook wouldn't come off. It was like a nightmare."

His mother smiled reassuringly. She was troubled, though. Perry had really been scared, and he didn't scare easily. She pushed back the hair from his forehead. "Do you feel any better?" she asked.

He flexed his hand. "Fine, I guess. Except for the memory, it's like it never happened."

"What never happened?" Jennifer demanded, bursting into the room. Edward and Jamie were close behind her.

"What's going on?"

"That was some scream."

"Calm down," cautioned their mother. "Perry had a little accident. Nothing for you to be concerned about. Why don't we all go check on your father? He can't be sleeping through so much commotion, and I'm sure he'd like the company."

Perry was the last one out. He bent down to retrieve the hook, but in doing so his gaze fell across the new scratch on his bedpost. How could a rubber hook do that to wood? Perry didn't know, but he left the hook where it was.

Professor Wynd was glad of the visit, though he wouldn't let the children approach him. "If I have a virus," he explained, "it might be contagious."

"How do you feel?" Edward asked.

"Pretty well. A little tired. I do have a question for all of you, however. Have any of you ever been too sick to do magic?"

They shook their heads.

"When I had the chickenpox," said Perry, "I conjured a spell to keep it from itching. But the spell didn't work. Is that what you mean?"

The professor smiled. "Not exactly. It's on the right track, though."

"You mean you can't do magic now, Father?" Jamie asked.

"Apparently not. The way I feel, I couldn't even pull a rabbit out of a hat." He grinned. "Perhaps it's your mother's influence."

"Certainly not," she retorted. "Don't tease them, Alexander. You can see they're upset."

"Your magic can't be gone," Jennifer insisted. It was an awful thought.

"I think not. After all, where would it go? We Wynds learn our spells, but we inherit the magic to do them. That's why the Old Magic is so special."

"But maybe because we inherit it," said Perry, "the magic is affected by sickness and stuff."

"Very likely," the professor agreed. "And with the care I'm getting, I'll be better in no time. I've been sleeping so much, though, I haven't spoken to Alison about her new job. How is she doing?"

The children shrugged awkwardly.

"She told me she was enjoying it," Mrs. Wynd

reported.

"She said the same to us," Edward remarked.

"Good. I'm looking forward to hearing about it. The experience should be interesting."

The children nodded. It would be interesting to say the least.

THIRTEEN

ALISON was halfway home when she stopped abruptly. The argument she was having with herself had reached a crucial point. Should she accept Miss Harding's word for everything? True, the conference members could be shy, and their meetings might be private and personal. And maybe the strange talk at the reception was not unusual from people who were drinking too much. Perhaps the "souvenirs" from the nature walk were nothing more than that.

The dead lizards were another matter. Alison tried to shrug them off, but her thoughts kept returning to them. And when she thought about them, all of her other doubts surfaced. If witches were gathering in Westbridge for some evil reason—there she was, thinking like Jennifer—Alison could not face them alone. Still, she also resisted the idea of simply running home for help. She would have to be absolutely positive. It was time to put her suspicions to the test.

THE ASSISTANT MANAGER looked up from the desk at Alison's arrival. "I thought you had gone home," he said sullenly.

"Oh, no, I was just running an errand." She did not mention that she had been waiting on the green for an hour.

"I see. Well, the conference has already begun its evening session."

Alison was prepared for this. "Of course," she said airily. "Miss Harding told me they might start before I returned. I'll join them now." She trotted off across the lobby.

"Miss Wynd!"

Alison turned.

"Miss Harding told me that the conference should not be disturbed for any reason."

"I know that. I'll make sure it isn't. Thank you."

The assistant manager shrugged. He was not about to start an argument on Miss Harding's behalf.

Alison left the lobby quickly. She did not head directly for the main door to the conference room, though. Instead, she went down a back hall. Amid all her shuttling at the inn, Alison had learned that every large room had a fire exit for emergencies. The one to the Harding conference was around the corner from the kitchen.

She found the door easily and reached for the knob. "It's eavesdropping for a good cause," she told herself. The knob, however, would not turn. Alison sighed. The door had no lock, but it wasn't used much. Living in an old house, Alison was used to sticky doors. And she had a good spell for dealing with them.

The door shuddered under the enchantment, but it stayed shut.

Alison tried it again with the same result. How sticky could the door be? "Put yourself in their shoes," she thought. "If you were a witch, would you leave an unlocked door unguarded?" Alison set about investigating this possibility. Sure enough, she soon detected a spell. The question was, could she break it?

She could. The spell had only been designed to stop curious, but ordinary, people. Obviously, the Hardings had not expected magical interference. Alison smiled.

The door opened silently into darkness. Beyond it a stage curtain blocked everything from view.

"More belladonna," she heard Jocelyn Grant say from the other side of it.

"And only a cup of the ground root," Max Gunther added. "I don't suppose you care to explain what we're making, Madeleine?"

Her voice sounded quite close. "You're making a recipe to my specifications. It includes things that you gathered today. The spell calls for some ingredients from the local setting in which it's conjured."

"Yes, yes," Max said heatedly. "But spell for *what?*"

"Patience, Max, patience. Tell me, you've each had a day to consider a use for the Old Magic. Any suggestions?"

"I have one," said Nathaniel Mandrake. "The Old Magic would give me the power to deal fiendishly with my enemies."

"I don't need much," said Sarah MacGregor. "Just enough to change my looks permanently. People expect such nice things of me on account of my face. For years I delighted in disappointing them. Yet even that grows tiresome."

Alison suddenly stiffened. Was she being watched? Fumbling for an explanation, she turned—and found herself staring at the white cat, Agatha.

Alison sighed in relief and closed the door.

"What are you doing here?" she whispered.

The cat growled.

"I guess you're right. Who am I to ask that?"

Agatha pushed her head against the door.

"I can't let you in. They'd wonder how you managed it."

Agatha arched her back and hissed.

"It's nothing personal. I'm sure. . . ."

Agatha did not stay to listen, but bounded away up the hall.

"I tried to be nice about it." Alison shrugged and opened the door again to listen.

Phoebe Tokla was giggling. "Could the Old Magic make the roads slippery on a dry night? Think of the accidents that would cause."

Max Gunther snorted. "Accidents, indeed. I am not here to engage in child's play."

Madeleine Harding rapped sharply on the podium. "That's where you're wrong, Max. Child's play is exactly what has brought us together. Your suggestions were nothing more than I anticipated. Only Phoebe proposed anything with real scope, however frivolous. The rest of you cannot see beyond your own petty concerns. That has been our problem for too long. Why must the grand scheme be outside our grasp? Think of our forebears, obeyed and feared, with tyrannical force."

"But that time has passed," said Jocelyn Grant. "The rise of science and education have—"

"Directed our fate until now," Madeleine continued fiercely. "We will endeavor to restore the balance."

"How?" asked Nathaniel Mandrake, voicing the question for everyone. "Speeches alone will not do the trick."

Madeleine smiled. "Not trick," she said, "but trick-or-treat. Tomorrow night is All Hallow's Eve, a night long revered by us. It is not honored now, cheapened by children collecting candy in silly costumes. Yet even in this travesty, our influence is felt. Monsters, ghosts, and other creatures of evil are popular disguises. What I propose is an extension of the children's own choices. We will conscript their innocent souls to usher in a new age."

"You still haven't said how," Max Gunther observed.

"Simply stated, by turning the children into the very creatures they imitate tomorrow night."

Alison's gasp was smothered by a bony hand gripping her jaw. She was yanked away from the door, which was silently shut. Her glance caught Agatha watching her smugly.

"So," hissed Nicholas Cudgel, holding her arm, "you chose to meddle, eh? That will prove to be a costly decision." He hesitated. "We will not disturb the conference now. The Hardings can deal with you later."

ALISON SAT GLUMLY on Mrs. Harding's bed. She had been sitting there for two hours, ever since Cudgel had escorted her upstairs. He had warned her against making a scene, and she hadn't, though not to please him. What good would it do to escape? She only knew the Hardings' goal, not the plan itself. She had to find out more. And she could only do that by staying put.

"How long are we going to sit here?" she asked.

Cudgel glared at her from a chair. "We wait for the Hardings to return. Now keep quiet or I'll bind and gag you."

Alison just barely managed to keep herself under control. Cudgel was looking for trouble, but it was too soon for her to act.

The sound of rapidly approaching footsteps distracted them both. Cudgel rose from his seat. Alison took a deep breath.

The door opened.

". . . for a moment I thought Max would explode. He looked—"

Madeleine Harding gaped at Alison. "Cudgel, what's the meaning of this? Shut the door, Amelia! Quickly!"

"Agatha found her eavesdropping on the conference," Cudgel explained. "I apprehended her listening at the fire door behind the curtain."

"Impossible," said Amelia. "I sealed that door."

Her mother leveled her gaze at Alison. "The proof says otherwise. This slip of a girl couldn't get past a seal."

Alison tried her best to look innocent. "Mother, I. . . ."

"Stop making excuses. It's too late for that. I was skeptical from the first about having an outsider among us. Tell me, Alison, what did you hear?"

"I don't mean to be disrespectful, but it sounded like a lot of mumbo-jumbo. I only did it because I admired you both and I wanted to learn something."

Madeleine frowned. "She seems guileless. Too guileless, perhaps. Had I expected this, I would have brought along the proper instruments. After a session with them, she would have spoken quite freely."

Alison blanched.

Amelia's eyes narrowed. "Obviously, we cannot let her go. You look surprised, Alison. Too bad. Remember, you brought this on yourself."

"Yes," said Madeleine. "Curiosity killed the cat, you know. You're much bigger than a cat." She tapped her cheek. "What do you suggest, Amelia? Hiring her was your idea."

"After tomorrow night, it won't matter what she knows or who she tells. We must keep her here till then. I will call her home and explain to her mother that Alison's duties have kept her working late. She will sleep here at the conference's expense. By the time anyone misses her, our work will be done."

"That seems like a lot of fuss, Amelia."

"We must not risk raising any suspicions. News of a missing girl would travel fast in a small town. We don't want to discourage any parents from sending out their children tomorrow night."

"And how do we keep the girl quiet?"

"A sleeping potion, I think. And Cudgel can watch over her. Don't make the potion too strong, though, Mother. We do want Alison to wake up again."

"Is that important?"

Alison certainly thought so.

"Of course, Mother. Alison has been a big

help to us. We wouldn't want her to miss the chance of appreciating your handiwork."

Mrs. Harding brightened. "An excellent point, Amelia. There are times when you make me proud. Cudgel, get my things."

"At once, Madam." He opened the closet door and pulled out a battered leather trunk.

Mrs. Harding passed her hand over the locks. The clasps sprang back. Carefully, she lifted the lid. The inside of the trunk was lined with slots and containers, each one holding a dusty bottle or flask. None of the liquids and powders were labeled, but she seemed familiar with them all.

"Does this interest you?" she said to Alison, who was gaping at the collection. "You're a plucky girl, I'll grant you that. It's a pity your first exposure to magic comes under such circumstances."

As she spoke, she mixed ingredients together in a small chalice. A pinch of this, a dab of that, two dollops of some crimson liquid—and the potion began to take shape. She mashed three roots with a mortar and pestle and threw them in. Great puffs of steam rose from the chalice, filling the room with a rancid odor.

Alison almost gagged.

"What a pleasant aroma," said Madeleine, stirring the potion. She dipped her finger in the bubbling brew, licked it, and yawned twice. "Just about ready," she remarked.

Alison wrinkled her nose. She had expected to be made a prisoner, not to be put to sleep. That complicated matters. At least the Hardings didn't suspect her of any magical knowledge, which meant she could still use magic to her advantage.

Madeleine noted Alison's hesitation. "Come, come," she said, "we have no time to waste. Do not worry. I gave up trying to make these painful years ago. Pain and sleep do not mix."

"Her lips are trembling," Amelia noted.

Madeleine loomed before Alison, pressing the chalice to her lips. "A prayer, maybe? It will make no difference. Drain the cup, child. I will not ask you twice."

Alison drank.

She was aware that the Hardings had backed away, but why should that set the room spinning like a merry-go-round. "Let me off," she pleaded. "I'm getting dizzy." She winced. "And it hurts."

"Yes, it does," Madeleine cackled. "I lied about the pain."

Faster and faster the room turned around. The Hardings, Cudgel, and the furniture all blurred against the walls. And then Alison closed her eyes, a small cry escaping her.

"She won't sleep for a hundred years," Madeleine observed, "but she'll sleep long enough."

FOURTEEN

JAMIE stumbled into the kitchen the next morning and yawned. "What's it like out?" he asked.

"Cold," said Edward, coming in behind him.

They sat down at the table and wrestled the cereal away from Perry.

Jennifer was making toast. "Alison better get down here soon," she said. "She's going to be late. We'll have to talk to her on the way to school. I fell asleep before she came in."

"So did I."

"Me, too."

Footsteps sounded on the stairs.

"Good morning," their mother said cheerily.

" 'Morning!" they chorused.

"How's Father?" asked Edward.

"Still sleeping. He's getting a lot of rest."

"So's Alison," said Jamie. "She's late."

"Alison isn't here," Mrs. Wynd told them. "Last night Miss Harding called up and asked if Alison could sleep at the inn. Apparently, one of their receptions ran late. Miss Harding was very apologetic. She insisted on giving Alison a room at the conference's expense."

"What did Alison say?" asked Jennifer.

"I didn't speak to her. Miss Harding explained that she was in the middle of telling the history of Westbridge to the participants."

The children exchanged glances.

Mrs. Wynd eyed them suspiciously. "You all look very serious."

"Must be the cereal," said Perry, holding up the box.

"I wonder what sleeping in the Westbridge Inn is like," said Edward. "I'll have to ask Alison at lunch."

"Speaking of lunch," said their mother, "pack one for her, too. Alison won't have a chance to make anything today."

The children were soon ready to leave. Mrs. Wynd helped them gather their books and saw them to the door. Then she watched as they huddled together on their way down the driveway. "I don't know what's going on," she mused, "but I'm sure they're up to something."

By the time Perry got out of school that afternoon, the others were already waiting for him. They did not look happy.

"What's wrong?" Perry asked.

Edward held up the extra lunch. "Alison wasn't in school today. And she said she wouldn't miss any school on this job."

"So now," said Jamie, "we have to find her."

The inn seemed the logical place to begin the search. The assistant manager was standing at the desk when the Wynds burst in upon him.

"Am I under attack?" he asked dryly.

"Of course not," said Perry. If the Wynds had been attacking him, he wouldn't have had to ask.

"We're looking for Alison Wynd," said Edward. "A tall girl with auburn hair."

"She works for the conference," Jamie added.

"What business do you have with Miss Wynd?"

"She's our sister," said Jennifer.

"I should have guessed. Miss Wynd was much in evidence over the weekend, but not today."

"When did you last see her?" asked Perry.

"Yesterday evening. She returned from an errand and went to the conference meeting."

"Where are the conference members now?" Jennifer asked.

"I do not keep track of them. Most of them, however, did go out a short time ago."

"Thanks," said Edward. He led the others back outside. "Look," he continued, "wherever these people are, Alison may be with them. Search the area and meet here again in an hour to report."

They scoured the town for any sign of the strangers. Several people had seen them, but no one had been paying much attention. After tracing down a bunch of false leads, the discouraged children gathered on the steps of the inn.

"Any luck at all?" asked Jennifer.

"I was told they headed north," said Jamie. "And east and south and west. It depended on who answered my question."

"I got dizzy from going around in circles," said Edward.

"Well, Alison doesn't have to be with them," muttered Perry. "They could be holding her in some castle dungeon."

"There are no castles in Westbridge," countered Jennifer.

Jamie glanced up at the second floor of the inn. "That's true, but. . . . Perhaps we've made this more difficult than it is. Follow me."

They reentered the lobby.

The assistant manager raised his head from

the ledger. "Ah," he said, "besieged once more."

"Can you tell us which room is Alison Wynd's?" Jamie asked. "She slept here last night."

"Impossible. She hasn't registered. No one sleeps in the Westbridge Inn without signing the ledger."

"The Hardings are registered, aren't they?" asked Edward.

"Certainly."

"Did they rent another room last night?"

The assistant manager checked. "Yes," he said, "in fact they did. Room twenty-eight. I understood they needed it for some private entertaining." He closed the ledger. "I think that's enough questions. I'm rather busy just now."

"Doing what?" asked Perry.

Edward nudged him. "You've been very helpful, sir. We won't trouble you further."

The others recognized Edward's tone at once. He was hatching a plan.

THE KNOCK at Room 28 brought a grizzled "Go away!" in response.

"Room service."

"Go away!" the voice shouted again. "I didn't order anything."

"Yes, sir. But I was told to pick up laundry."

"Laundry? What laundry? Can't you read the sign?"

"Sign? What sign?"

The door cracked open. An eye peered at him from inside. "The *Do Not Disturb* sign," said Nicholas Cudgel. "It's on the doorknob."

The doorknob was bare.

"Who are you, boy? I haven't seen you around the inn."

"I'm new here. Could I step in for a moment? Perhaps someone called without telling—"

"No one called. I'm not feeling well, and I don't appreciate these interruptions. I've already told the maid that. Now I'm telling you!"

The door slammed shut.

Edward stood in the hall, thinking. He pulled the *Do Not Disturb* sign from his pocket and returned to the stairs. The others were impatiently waiting for him. "A man is there," he told them. "A nasty man who could well be hiding something."

"Or someone," said Perry.

"Could we tempt him out?" wondered Jamie.

Edward shook his head. "I doubt it. He seems like the suspicious type."

"You know," mused Jennifer, "it's not surprising such people are unfriendly. Cooped up all day with only their own miserable thoughts for company. This poor fellow sounds as if he could use our help."

"What kind of *help*?" asked Edward.

"The PTA is sponsoring a Halloween dance tonight at the high school. We should send him there."

"He won't go," said Perry. "You heard what Edward said."

Jennifer smiled. "I didn't say we should give him a choice."

NICHOLAS CUDGEL sat upright in a wingback chair, watching the last wisps of sunset withdraw. He hated sunsets. The soft array of pastel colors was disgustingly cheerful. Shadows were more to his taste.

Alison stirred slightly on the bed. Cudgel was surprised she moved at all. The potion had been a strong one.

Tap. Tap. Tap.

Cudgel looked down. His foot was shaking. He wondered if his nerves were finally beginning to show. Before the night was old, the world would be a very different place. Madeleine Harding was ushering in a new Dark Age. Cudgel grunted with satisfaction. He was going to feel right at home.

Tap, tap, tap, tap, tap.

Now both of Cudgel's feet were moving, and in a distinct rhythm. Cudgel tried to hold them still. Then his hands began to twitch. A tingling sensation crept up his legs, propelling him out of the chair.

In another minute, Cudgel was prancing about the room, dancing a waltz with an imaginary partner. His movements were awkward; anger and dismay radiated from his face. But he couldn't stop. The waltz gave way to a polka, sending him flailing around in a circle. Several times he grabbed a bedpost in passing. Fingers trembling, his hands refused to hold on, and off he went again.

A theatrical soft shoe routine was next. Only now he found himself shuffling toward the door. He opened it, and continued into the hall.

The assistant manager was a veteran hotel employee, but never before had he seen a gangly man dance down the stairs and sashay out of a lobby. And Mr. Cudgel had seemed like such a quiet sort. Ah, well, one couldn't ever be sure with guests.

Once Cudgel had left the hall, Perry and Edward emerged from a broom closet. Jamie and Jennifer joined them from another one around the corner.

"He'll make the PTA proud," said Jennifer.

"With or without a partner."

Jamie looked toward the open room. "Let's find out what he's hiding."

They rushed to the door. "Alison!" they cried, seeing her lying on the bed.

"I hope we don't have to kiss her," said Perry.

But unlike Sleeping Beauty, Alison simply sat up and laughed. "Oh," she said, "it was so hard keeping a straight face. I figured you were behind the dancing. Boy, was he mad."

"Are you all right?" asked Jamie.

"Yes. They gave me a sleeping potion last night, but I was able to lessen its effect." She yawned. "Pretty well, anway. If you hadn't come along, I would have had to do something myself. We've got to stop them."

"Hah!" triumphed Jennifer. "Then we were right."

Alison blushed. "Yes, yes, and I'm sorry I doubted you. But being right doesn't solve our problems. Wait till you hear what the witches are planning. They're going to change the children of Westbridge into whatever creatures they disguise themselves as tonight. Once a few monsters are running loose, they in turn will infect others."

"Plastic and paper turning into the real thing?" said Jamie. "That's hard to believe."

Perry gasped. "It explains my hook, though."

"What explains your hook?" demanded Jennifer.

He told them what had happened the night before.

"Mother thought it was an accident," said Edward. "But apparently you triggered something in the hook itself."

"Why didn't you tell us?" asked Jamie.

"I wanted to forget about it. I wasn't proud of what happened. I thought it was my own fault."

"You were lucky Mother came in," said Jennifer. "The spell broke when you hugged her."

"But Mother can't be everywhere tonight," said Edward. "And if the hook was specially prepared, probably all the costumes were. Mr, Dickinson did say he had a new supplier this year. What was his name, Perry? Cuddle?"

"Not Cudgel!" exclaimed Alison.

"That's it. How did you know?"

"You just sent Nicholas Cudgel dancing into town."

It took a moment for them to absorb this.

"They certainly have things carefully arranged," said Jamie. "Still, even with treated costumes, it will take a lot of power to make so many permanent transformations."

"How big is the conference?" asked Jennifer.

"Thirteen people."

"That might be enough," said Edward.

"Oh," Alison added, "they also mentioned having captured some of the Old Magic. That will help."

"Around here?" said Perry. "If there were any Old Magic in Westbridge, woudn't we know about it?"

"We do," said Jennifer. "We're of the Old Magic."

Jamie bit his lip. "So is Father. . . ."

"And he got sick passing through town," remembered Jennifer.

Perry was furious. "They can't do that to my father and get away with it."

"We have plenty of reasons to stop them," said Edward. "But we must find them first."

"That won't be hard," said Alison. "They've been meeting in the same room every night."

"Maybe," he replied. "We were told the conference members had gone out."

"Look!" cried Perry, pointing to the window.

A procession of cats was crossing the driveway. Agatha was in the lead, the others following at a respectful distance.

"Where are they going?" wondered Jamie.

Alison put on her coat. "There's only one way to find out."

FIFTEEN

MADELEINE HARDING was well-pleased with her surroundings. Weathered gravestones the size of croquet wickets studded the ground at her feet. Scattered leaves swirled about them, refugees from the barren trees overhead. These trees ringed the sky, their branches sending crooked shadows slinking along the moonlit landscape.

"It is a fit night out for man and beast," she declared.

Her hooded and cloaked companions murmured their agreement.

"Especially for the beasts," she noted. "We come now to our final challenge, the moment of our glory. As a precaution, we will protect ourselves against any interruptions. It is important that we not be disturbed. Two measures should suffice. First, a Wind of Confusion. . . ."

She waved her arms in an arc. A sudden gust sprang up, blowing outward in every direction. "Second, we will post sentries during the preliminaries. Between the two, we will be secure."

THE WYNDS were almost across the green when the warm breeze wafted by them.

"Keep a sharp lookout," said Jennifer. "Those cats will be hard to see in the dark."

"What cats?" asked Perry.

Jennifer blinked. "You idiot. The ones we're . . . we're. . . . What time is it?"

Edward glanced at his watch. "Just after five. You know, I should be getting home. My party's at eight o'clock. I have to get ready."

"Me, too," said Jamie. "My costume takes a while to put on."

Only Alison plunged ahead. She had a score to settle with the Hardings, which strengthened her determination. "Come on," she called out. "We don't have time to waste."

"She's right," said Edward. "At this rate, I'll barely be able to eat dinner and change."

"I should be trick-or-treating already," said Perry.

Jennifer sat down on the grass. "I'm sleepy," she announced.

Alison stalked up to them. "What's wrong with you all? We have to follow the cats."

"Why?" asked Jamie. "I don't like cats."

Alison shuddered as another waft of air blew past her. How could she have left the inn? Miss Harding was depending on her. No, that wasn't true. It should be. The conference wasn't over.

Alison shook her head. "Something's wrong here. Where were we going?"

Edward looked at his watch again.

Perry and Jamie shrugged.

"Beats me," said Jennifer.

"I'm going home," said Edward. "Anyone else coming?"

"Sure," said Jamie.

"I will," said Perry.

Jennifer yawned. "I'm going to take a nap."

"Not here," said Perry. He reached out to pull her up.

"Ow!" she cried. "Don't squeeze so hard. That hand still hurts where the cat scratched it."

"Cats!" exclaimed Alison. "Weren't we doing something with cats?"

Jennifer rubbed her hand. "That's right. We were following them. But there was more to it, I think."

"Concentrate," said Edward. "We can remember if we try hard enough."

"The witches!" exclaimed Perry.

"And Halloween!" cried Alison.

"How could we forget?" asked Jamie.

"There's a smell of magic in the air," said Edward. "Maybe we had some help. We'd better protect ourselves against its happening again."

"Hurry, hurry," Alison said impatiently. "It's getting dark."

The children ran on in the direction they had last seen the cats take.

"How will we find them now?" asked Perry. "They could be anywhere."

"Not anywhere," Alison maintained. "Someplace special."

"If I were a witch," said Jamie, "where would I go?"

"You'd make a silly witch," said Jennifer. "But you might end up in a cave."

"Not out this way," said Jamie. "There aren't any hills, just a few houses, the post road, the old graveyard, and—"

"Of course!" said Alison. "A graveyard would be perfect."

Jennifer shuddered. "Perfect for them, maybe. It gives me the creeps."

"And that," said Edward, "is what Halloween is all about."

On a ridge facing the post road, a hooded figure stood silhouetted against the gray sky. Her dimpled face was hidden in shadows. "Boring," she muttered, gazing into the darkness. "Boring, boring, boring."

In the gloom of the trees below, the Wynds watched warily.

"Can we go around?" whispered Jamie.

Edward frowned. "They probably have several guards. We'll just have to get by one."

"But without being seen," said Alison. "We don't want the sentry sounding the alarm. Any ideas?"

"It should be confusing," reasoned Jennifer. "Something that will make the sentry curious, but not concerned."

Perry reached into his pocket. "How about this?" he asked, taking out the drummer he had fixed in school. The drumhead had been neatly replaced, and the soldier looked ready for action.

"It might work," said Edward. "That is, with a little help from its friends."

The sentry was startled when a crisp drum roll interrupted the quiet night sounds she expected to hear. She peered down toward the road, searching for its source. No one was visible, but the drum roll continued. Was this a danger or merely some kind of prank? But what

harm could come from a drum roll? The sentry slowly descended from her post. She welcomed the chance to match wits with a prankster.

"Close enough?" whispered Edward.

Alison nodded.

The sentry ignored the leaves swirling at her feet until they rose up and swarmed upon her. She fell back in dismay. Hundreds and hundreds of leaves continued the attack. In vain, she tried to cry out. The leaves pressed against her mouth, and the sheer weight of them drove her to the ground. She staggered up, only to begin spinning like a top. Around and around she twirled, churning the air like a small tornado. At last, she fell down in a heap.

The leaves settled at her side.

The children approached cautiously.

"It's Phoebe Tokla," said Alison.

"The one at the farmstand, I think," Jennifer added. "She's going to wake up tomorrow with an awful headache."

"Let's go," said Edward. "We still have twelve to go."

Alison lingered a moment in thought, and then hurried to catch up with the others.

As THE WITCHES finished gathering wood for the fire, the cats made their appearance.

"Clever Agatha," purred Madeleine. "You have arrived in time to witness my triumph."

Agatha jumped up on the nearest sizable gravestone. Her companions found perches of their own.

"I think we are ready, Amelia."

Her daughter removed the lantern from beneath her cloak. She placed it above the cauldron and removed her hand. The lantern remained suspended in midair. Its light blazed outward, bathing the assembled witches in its glow. Only barest hint of light reached the rocks where the Wynds sat huddled together.

"I count nine," said Alison. "There must be three other sentries besides Phoebe."

Edward sighed. "Not the best odds, even with the element of surprise."

"Could we foil the spell from here?" asked Jennifer.

"How?" said Jamie. "We don't know anything about it."

"You don't," Alison murmured, "but I . . . I have an idea. There's no time to explain. It's something I have to do alone. Try to delay them as long as possible. Good luck."

"You can't leave so—" began Jennifer. She stopped protesting. Alison had gone.

"Should we follow her?" asked Perry.

Edward shook his head. "Let's hope she knows what she's doing. Delaying them will be enough of a problem for us."

"It's funny," said Jamie, "that they bother with that lantern when they have such a roaring fire. I mean, it's a good trick making it hover, but why go to the trouble?"

"It is peculiar," Jennifer agreed. "And that isn't all that's odd. When I look at the lantern, the light makes me feel the way I do when Father does a spell. The air tingles somehow."

"I know what you mean," said Edward. He scratched his head. "Perhaps it's not an ordinary lantern. They must be keeping the Old Magic nearby. What if the lantern is holding it?"

"Lanterns can break," Perry said simply.

"True," said Jamie. "And that would cause confusion."

Jennifer nodded. "And confusion means delay." She rubbed the scratch on her hand. "I have some unfinished business to settle with those cats. Maybe we can enlist their help."

"How?" asked Perry.

"Follow my lead."

The cats had watched the preparations with great intensity. They sensed the importance of the moment. Their tails twitched in excitement. Still, the wait was making them hungry.

Their opal eyes widened as the heat from the fire rippled around the lantern. The air shimmered and the lantern shifted size and shape. In its place was a milk can.

The cats wailed in surprise.

"What's wrong with the cats?" wondered Amelia. She followed their gaze to the lantern. Nothing seemed amiss.

"Perhaps the ceremony affects them," said Madeleine.

The cats wailed again, their tails now twitching uncontrollably. They were not going to lose another milk can. With a glance at one another, they tensed for a spring.

And jumped.

The spell holding the lantern aloft was not meant to withstand such an impact. The lantern fell to the ground under the cats' combined weight. The glass shattered. Before the witches could react, the luminescence inside rose like the vapor from a candle and vanished.

The cats howled all the louder, sniffing angrily at the metal frame and shards of glass. They had been robbed again. Of what use to them was a broken lantern?

Madeleine Harding trembled in her fury. "Treachery!" she shouted. "Treachery from within. This was no time for games. Even you,

Agatha, even you betrayed me."

The cats paid no attention to her ranting.

"No apology?" she fumed. "No contriteness? You will pay dearly for your actions." She stared at the unhappy creatures.

The wailing stopped. The cats had turned to stone.

Up among the rocks, the Wynds were well-satisfied with their work.

"That did it," said Edward. "And we're still in the clear."

"What next?" asked Perry.

"You will join the gathering below," said an ominous voice from behind them.

The children whirled to find Cudgel and three sentries at their backs.

"Run!" cried Jamie.

But they couldn't run. They could barely move.

"Give up," Cudgel ordered. "The harder you try to escape, the more you are bound." He pointed a crooked finger at Edward. "You are the boy from the inn. We have a score to settle. I don't enjoy playing the fool."

A sentry shoved Jennifer forward. "Do not force us to take harsher measures."

Sighing deeply, the children descended into the graveyard.

SIXTEEN

THE WITCHES gathered around the shattered lantern, their faces reflecting their disappointment.

"My poor foolish Circe," said Jocelyn Grant.

"What now, Madeleine?" Nathaniel Mandrake asked bitterly. "Changing cats to stone will not bring back the Old Magic."

"Could we recapture it?" wondered Max Gunther.

"I fear not," said Amelia. "The lantern had been specially prepared for its function. The Old Magic is not easily contained."

"Will you speak, Madeleine?" asked Sarah MacGregor.

Madeleine had lowered her head following her revenge upon the cats. Now she slowly raised it. "The loss is a grave setback," she admitted, "but we are not beaten yet. I have worked too long to acknowledge defeat now. The Old Magic would have made our task simpler and more certain." She paused. "Without it, I must take a greater risk. I will feed my own spirit into the spell, even as I did the other night. This will mean a change in the plan, however. You, Amelia, will have to put the ingredients in the cauldron itself as I call for them. I will be too absorbed to manage that."

"Yes, Mother."

"Make no mistakes or the spell will go awry."

"I will not fail you."

Her mother nodded. "Then call in the sentries."

"Hold!" Cudgel called out. He entered their midst leading the Wynds in tow. The witches stepped aside, grumbling among themselves at his new interruption.

"Explain yourself, Cudgel!" Madeleine demanded. "Why have you brought these children here?"

"I did not bring them, Madam. They were watching from the ridge."

"I see. And what were you doing there?"

"I was forced out of the inn"—he cleared his throat—"by a compulsion to dance. I ended up at some social gathering before I could bring it under control." He pointed at Edward. "This boy had something to do with it. He was snooping around just before it happened. I thought it more important to warn you than to keep guarding the girl. It seems these children preceded me."

Nathaniel Mandrake glanced sharply at Perry. "Don't I know you, boy?"

Perry shook his head.

The warlock snapped his fingers. "Of course! You were spying on us yesterday in the woods. Quite a conspiracy is developing. Well, I know how to deal with spies."

"I was there, too," Jamie said stoutly. "You'll have to deal with us both."

"And us," Edward and Jennifer chorused.

Nathaniel grinned wickedly. "As you wish," he said. "The more the merrier."

"Wait," cautioned Cudgel. "There is more. From what we overheard the children say, they were responsible for something to do with the cats."

Madeleine Harding tensed. "What? Was I too preoccupied to notice? What did you do, children? An illusion, perhaps? It appears I blamed my beloved Agatha unjustly. You will suffer for that."

"What should we do with them?" Cudgel asked.

She gestured impatiently. "We will question them later. For now, they will make a fitting audience. After all, it is their friends who will lead us back to power. But just to make sure we have no more audience participation, surround them with a Wall."

The sentries herded the Wynds into a clearing and etched a deep line in the ground around them. Cudgel inspected it briefly. He and the sentries then returned to the others.

Jennifer was insulted. "Aren't they going to watch us? We're dangerous, you know."

"Maybe they don't have to," said Edward. He extended his hands outward above the line at his feet. "This Wall they mentioned is a solid barrier." He pushed against it. "Invisible and strong."

"Can we break it?" asked Jamie.

"We can try."

While they each made their own tests, the witches began to chant. Most of them stood near the cauldron. A few passed by the ingredients. One hooded figure did this very carefully.

"We are all here," said Madeleine. "And it will take our full strength to compensate for the Old Magic. Start the fire, Sarah."

The kindling blazed up at Sarah MacGregor's command.

Madeleine raised her arms and spoke:

The enchantment will begin forsooth,
With eagle's claw and serpent's tooth.

Both ingredients were dropped into the cauldron. The fire blazed higher.

Then scattered dust from ancient tombs,
And silken strands from spider looms.

Amelia emptied a jar quickly and scraped the
spider webs out of a pouch.

With lizards' tongues and fine ground bones,
Add poisoned roots and dismal moans.

Most of the onlookers shivered in delight at
the horrid sounds. The Wynds just shuddered.

"That woman doesn't count very well," muttered Jennifer. "They're one short and she didn't
even notice."

"Unfortunately," said Edward, "she counts
fine. I checked."

"How can that be?"

"It doesn't matter now," said Jamie. "They're
not even weakened. We have to break free."

"I'm trying," said Edward. "In another
hour. . . ."

"We don't have that long," Jennifer guessed. "Maybe I can slow them down."

"Wait, Jen," cautioned Perry. "It might not. . . ."

But Jennifer wasn't waiting. A watter ball appeared in her hand and she threw it at the fire. The water ball splattered against the Wall, drenching Edward, who was kneeling at its base.

Perry shook his head.

Madeleine Harding glimpsed this effort through the rising smoke. She smiled and continued.

> Ferrets' eyes and wing of bat,
> Shattered dreams and dragon fat.

The latter hissed loudly as it was poured in, like a thousand angry snakes.

With a final flourish, Madeleine Harding proclaimed:

> The spell is strong, its focus dour,
> Let it now commence the Witching Hour.

The cauldron brew bubbled furiously, churning itself into a raging tempest. The witches crowded closer, all except one, who chose that moment to back away.

Suddenly the mixture subsided. A sweet mist

rose from the slimy mass.

"Ahhhh!" cried the witches, savoring the smell.

"Fools!" Madeleine shouted. "The mist should be sour, not sweet. Something is wrong. I must correct the error." She closed her eyes, the strain pulling her face taut.

Not one bubble reappeared. The brew had jelled.

By now the cauldron fumes had engulfed the witches. Since the smell was not the proper one, it did not have the proper effect. Max Gunther hiccupped. The rest lurched about like drunken revelers.

"Noooooo!" Madeleine gasped. She put forth all her strength.

Amelia wagged a finger at her. "Careful, Mother," she said tipsily. "You're fading."

"Noooooooooooooo!" Madeleine wailed again.

And then she was gone.

But the witches were not paying attention. "Ha, ha!" cried Sarah MacGregor, gesturing at three companions.

Their cloaks fell away, and three moths fluttered into the night.

Amid sparks, flashes, and gleeful shouts, the witches all turned on one another. The spell had clouded their reason. In only moments, a succession of toads, lizards, and birds were fleeing the graveyard. As the fumes dispersed, the last surviors—Nathaniel Mandrake and Max Gunther—changed each other into owls and flew off in search of fieldmice.

"Well . . ." began Edward.

"Yes," said Jennifer, who was at something of a loss herself.

Jamie and Perry simply nodded.

Edward reached out cautiously. "The Wall is gone. We're free." He looked around in confusion. "I wonder what went wrong. They seemed to have things so precisely planned."

"So they did," said a hooded figure, emerging from the shadows.

"Oh, oh!" exclaimed Jamie. "Here we go again."

The stranger pulled back her cowl. Phoebe Tokla's curly hair and dimpled face shone forth in the moonlight.

"You should be asleep," said Perry.

"Look," said Jennifer.

Phoebe's features had grown suddenly misty. Her face blurred. And changed.

"Alison!" they cried.

She laughed and took a bow. "Trick-or-treat," she said.

PROFESSOR AND MRS. WYND were sitting in the kitchen when their children burst in upon them.

"Father, you look better," said Perry.

"Not better, completely well. About two hours ago, I felt fine again." He waved toward the cabinet, and all the glasses rattled their approval. "It must be that sturdy Wynd constitution."

"Partly, at least," murmured Edward.

"Where have you been?" asked their mother. "I see no costumes or candy. Yet you all look very pleased with yourselves."

"It started with the cats," began Jennifer.

"Actually, before that," said Alison.

"The costumes were ready months ago," Perry put in.

Their parents heard the whole story twice, and parts of it three times, before they had it straight.

"We would have been home sooner," said Jamie, "but we had to deal with the witches' luggage."

Perry laughed. "That was fun. We sent all the suitcases sailing out the windows back to their home addresses."

"The sudden exit will seem mysterious," said Alison, "but it's appropriate for Halloween."

"Quite a tale," their father mused. "Don't you agree, Elizabeth?"

She smiled. "It's safe to say that. Still, I'm sorry your first job turned out this way, Alison."

"It's not a total loss. The manager hinted that he'd hire me himself for the next conference. Fortunately for him, the Hardings paid in advance."

"Let's hope the next conference is less controversial," said Professor Wynd. "I don't fancy ever losing my magic again. It sounds, though, as if that knowledge may have disappeared with Madeleine Harding."

Everyone hoped so.

"What's the matter, Perry?" asked Edward. "You still look puzzled."

Perry frowned. "I'm just not sure why the witches' spell went so wrong."

"You should," said Alison. "I got the idea from what you did at dinner the other night. After I disguised myself as Phoebe, I gathered up some dirt and rocks, making them look like the ingredients I had seen in the kitchen. While everyone was distracted by your arrival, I made a few switches. That changed the spell considerably."

Perry nodded slowly. "Then I guess I deserve a lot of the credit."

"Only your usual small share," growled Jennifer.

"Now, Jen," said their mother, "allow him that consolation for the night's losses."

"Very well." She sniffed. "Though I shouldn't be so charitable. This time I would have embarrassed him and his dumb pirate costume."

Jamie sighed. "Tonight we got tricks instead of treats."

"True," said Perry, glancing defiantly at Jennifer. "But wait till next year."